The WEIGHT *of* BELONGING

The WEIGHT *of* BELONGING

BELLA DAVIS

Andborough Publishing
An Independent Publisher Since 2006

Publisher's Cataloging-in-Publication Data

Davis, Bella 1960–
The Weight of Belonging / Bella Davis.
— First edition.
p. cm.
ISBN: 979-8-9912582-7-2

    1. Historical fiction. 2. Victorian romance. 3. Journalists—Fiction. 4. Horse trainers—Fiction. 5. Secrets—Fiction. 6. Love stories. I. Title.
PS3604.D38 S65 2025
813'.6 — dc23
LCCN: 2025904819

Printed in the United States of America
10 9 8 7 6 5 4 3 2 1

Dedication

To my dearest children,

In the gentle hope that you shall ever cherish the virtues of kindness, courage, and wit, I dedicate these humble pages to you. May your hearts remain as lively as your imaginations, your laughter as bright as the morning sun, and your spirits undaunted by the trials of this ever-unpredictable world.

If this tale offers you but a moment's delight, a glimmer of amusement, or the smallest lesson in love, perseverance, or belonging, then I shall consider my task most excellently rewarded.

With all my affection and endless admiration,

I remain, ever yours.

Prologue

There were moments—fractured slivers of time—when Lucas Wycliffe almost believed he could outrun the past.

In the early light of dawn, when the mist clung low to the earth and the hills of Hawthorne Manor stood cloaked in quiet solitude, he could pretend. Pretend that he was not the man who had lost everything. That the echoes of failure didn't haunt him with every breath, every heartbeat, every shadow that crossed his path.

But the past had sharp teeth. And it never truly let go.

He stood at the edge of the paddock, the cold bite of morning air cutting through his coat, hands curled tightly around the rough wood of the fence. Beyond him, the horses grazed lazily—creatures of habit and grace, untouched by regret. Unburdened by memory.

He envied them.

The silence of the land was his penance—each dawn spent

with nothing but the weight of what could not be undone. The accident. Jacob's fall. The shattering of a future that had once been so certain.

Five years.

Five years of pretending that solitude was a choice, not a cage of his own making.

The villagers had long since stopped whispering when he passed. Pity had grown stale in their eyes, replaced by cautious respect or, worse, indifference. It was easier that way. Easier to be forgotten by a world that had once demanded too much of him.

And yet…

As the wind shifted, carrying with it the faint scent of earth and coming rain, a new dread settled in his chest. A whisper of change—unseen, unspoken—lurking just beyond the horizon.

He didn't know it yet.

But she was coming.

A woman with ink-stained fingers and sharp eyes that saw too much.

A woman who would walk straight into the quiet fortress he had built—

And tear it down from the inside.

Emma Ainsworth would be the storm he had spent his whole life running from.

And this time?

There would be nowhere left to hide.

Chapter One

The carriage wheels rumbled over the uneven country road, jostling Emma Ainsworth slightly as she peered out of the window. The rolling hills of Somersetshire framed the village of Dunster like a timeless painting, untouched by the passing decades. A long gravel drive led up to Hawthorne Manor, its stately presence softened only by the expanse of lush pastures and the well-maintained stables at its side.

Her destination.

And the home of Mr. Lucas Wycliffe.

Emma straightened her spine, drawing in a measured breath. She had engaged with men of influence before—politicians whose words were veiled in caution, merchants who hoarded their dealings as one does gold, and scholars who paraded their intellect as though it were a weapon.

But she suspected Mr. Wycliffe would prove an altogether different challenge.

A man of considerable means but little regard for society, he had turned away from the bustling life of London years ago, retreating instead to his stables, his lands, his solitude. Yet his work had drawn attention. His skill in breeding and rehabilitating horses had become a topic of admiration—even mystery—among equestrians and nobles alike.

And she was determined to uncover the truth.

The carriage slowed to a stop before the main house, the scent of fresh hay and damp earth mingling with the crisp autumn air. Emma stepped down, adjusting the hem of her traveling coat, before smoothing her gloved hands over the leather-bound notebook she carried.

A gentleman stood not far from the stables, his figure silhouetted against the dusk. His coat hung open, revealing the rough edges of a man accustomed to labor, not leisure. His boots bore the marks of a man who spent more time upon the earth than within drawing rooms, and his hands—strong, weathered—rested upon the wooden fence as he observed a dark stallion within the paddock.

Emma stepped forward, clearing her throat delicately. "Mr. Wycliffe?"

The man did not turn.

Undeterred, she tried again. "Mr. Lucas Wycliffe?"

This time, he shifted, casting her a glance over his

shoulder.

The first thing she noted was his gaze—piercing, assessing, and offering no easy interpretation His expression, however, remained carefully neutral, revealing neither curiosity nor welcome.

"Who is asking?" His voice was deep, even, yet edged with suspicion.

Emma lifted her chin. "Emma Ainsworth. I am a journalist, sent to write a feature upon your fine establishment." She extended a gloved hand in greeting.

"If it is flattery you seek to pen, Miss Ainsworth, you have come to the wrong place."

She blinked. "I beg your pardon?"

Lucas turned fully then, the full weight of his gaze settling upon her as though she were nothing more than an unfortunate disturbance.

"I do not entertain journalists," he said simply. Then, as though the matter were settled, he turned back toward the stallion.

Emma pressed her lips together, exhaling through her nose. She had anticipated a certain level of resistance, but she had not expected to be dismissed so summarily.

"You presume much, sir, and yet know nothing of my true intentions." Her voice remained steady, though her pulse quickened. "It is not my desire to write frivolous gossip, Mr. Wycliffe. My focus is upon industry and innovation—how small enterprises such as yours impact the greater community."

"I see no purpose in having my work dissected for the curiosity of others."

Emma squared her shoulders. "Then perhaps you might consider that your work speaks for itself—and that people might benefit from learning about it."

Lucas scoffed lightly, shaking his head. "I have no need for notoriety, Miss Ainsworth."

She hesitated, catching the flicker of something in his expression—discomfort, perhaps even regret.

Intriguing.

"You distrust the press, that much is clear," she said, watching him carefully. "But what if I prove myself? What if I earn the right to tell your story?"

Lucas turned back toward her then, arms crossed over his chest, expression unreadable. "And how do you propose to do that?"

Emma gestured toward the stables. "By working."

A flicker of amusement touched his lips before it was swiftly concealed. "You wish to play stable hand in exchange for an interview?"

Emma lifted her chin. "I am not above effort, Mr. Wycliffe. Should you fear my words might misrepresent your work, then permit me to observe it with my own eyes."

He studied her, the silence stretching between them, broken only by the occasional snort of a restless horse.

Then, at last, his mouth quirked slightly—just the

barest hint of amusement.

"Very well."

Emma straightened slightly, victorious. "Then we have an agreement?"

Lucas quirked a brow, the expression doing little to soften his otherwise rugged features. "Not quite. We have a test, Miss Ainsworth."

She arched a brow. "A test?"

Lucas stepped toward the stable, pausing at the entrance. "You would claim to understand this work? Then, Miss Ainsworth, you shall rise with the dawn and acquaint yourself with it properly."

Emma nodded. "I shall be here."

Lucas inclined his head slightly, then turned away, dismissing her without another word.

Emma exhaled slowly, adjusting the strap of her satchel as she turned back toward the manor.

He thought to scare her off, she realized.

But Lucas Wycliffe was about to learn that she was not so easily deterred.

✤

Chapter Two

The scent of damp hay and aged wood filled the cavernous stable, mingling with the unmistakable pungency of its less pleasant occupants. Sunlight streamed through the narrow slats in the wooden walls, illuminating the floating dust in golden shafts of morning light. The great beams of the stable arched above Emma Ainsworth's head, framing the long aisle of stalls with a kind of rustic symmetry.

Yet, for all its old-world charm, the air held an unmistakable earthy aroma, one that caused her to reconsider, for the briefest of moments, the wisdom of her decision.

She had expected labor. She had not expected this.

Emma stood at the threshold, adjusting the fastenings of her traveling cloak, her leather gloves clenched tightly in her fingers as she surveyed the scene before her. A row of stalls lined either side of the central walkway, each occupied by a great beast of sinew and strength, their large eyes observing her with idle curiosity. Several stable hands moved about their work in practiced rhythm, the scrape of rakes and the soft murmur of voices creating a quiet symphony of toil.

As she stepped forward, one of the grooms glanced up from where he stood brushing a chestnut mare. Upon seeing Lucas, he gave a brief nod of acknowledgment before returning to his task. His gaze barely flickered toward Emma before dismissing her entirely.

And there, standing with all the ease of a man who had no intention of lifting so much as a finger to assist her, was Mr. Lucas Wycliffe.

He leaned against a wooden pillar, arms crossed over his broad chest, the very picture of unbothered amusement. His shirtsleeves were rolled to his elbows, revealing forearms that bore the sun's bronzing and the marks of honest work. A single strand of dark hair had fallen across his forehead, but if he had noticed, he had made no attempt to push it away.

His posture suggested indifference. His expression, however, told a different tale—one of undeniable amusement.

Emma set her jaw.

"Surely, you are not in earnest."

Lucas did not move. "I assure you, Miss Ainsworth, I am not."

She cast a glance down the row of stalls, each more

offensively foul than the last. The straw lay sodden in places, darkened by dampness she did not care to name. The acrid sting of ammonia bit the air, curling in her throat.

Lucas shifted slightly, tilting his head in quiet, almost lazy satisfaction. "You wished to earn your interview," he reminded her. "This is the work that must be done."

Emma released a slow, measured breath, summoning all the patience she possessed.

She had spent long nights interrogating London's most obstinate politicians, had stood her ground in rooms filled with men who had dismissed her as inconsequential, and had waded through the relentless world of publishing, where she had been underestimated at every turn.

Surely, one insufferable horseman and a few piles of filth could not defeat her.

"I was under the impression I would be working with the horses."

Lucas pushed off the beam, his booted steps slow, deliberate—like a man far too entertained by his own game. "And so you shall. But first, you will see to their stalls."

He lifted a brow, as if daring her to object.

"Unless, of course, you have changed your mind?"

Ah. The challenge.

Emma knew it well—had encountered it a hundred times before. It was the same expression she had seen on the faces of men who had believed she would falter, that she would turn and walk away, conceding to the unspoken rule that some places, some tasks, were not meant for women.

She had never backed down then.

And she would not do so now.

Lifting her chin, she strode forward, her steps crisp, decisive. She reached for the pitchfork that leaned against the wall, its wooden handle smooth with years of use.

She had debated politics with the finest minds in London, had defended her position in drawing rooms filled with men twice her age, yet here, in the unceremonious grime of a stable, she found herself fighting a far different battle. One against mud, sweat, and the insufferable smirk of Lucas Wycliffe.

"Which stall first?"

Lucas's mouth quirked slightly—just enough to betray his surprise.

Then, with the air of a man bestowing a great privilege, he gestured toward the foulest, most wretched stall in sight.

Of course.

The straw was soaked through, its scent enough to make her eyes water.

She fought the urge to recoil, to press a gloved hand to her nose.

Instead, she tightened her grip upon the pitchfork and stepped forward.

She would not falter.

And Lucas Wycliffe would not have the satisfaction of seeing her retreat.

At first, the labor was strenuous but manageable. Emma had anticipated the effort required—physical work did not daunt her. With determination, she lifted each sodden heap of straw, tossing it into the waiting barrow. The damp fabric of her sleeves clung uncomfortably to her skin, and the sting of exertion pricked at her muscles, but she pressed on.

Yet, as the minutes passed, her movements slowed. The weight of the rake grew heavier in her grasp. Her muscles, unaccustomed to such labor, began to protest.

Emma paused briefly, brushing the back of her gloved hand across her forehead. A damp curl escaped its pin and fell against her cheek, clinging there as she exhaled.

From across the stable, Lucas Wycliffe observed her— his arms crossed, expression unreadable.

Emma's eyes narrowed slightly. "Are you merely going to stand there and observe?"

Lucas lifted a brow, his expression one of mock innocence. "You're doing quite well."

His utter disregard for her sarcasm sent a flicker of irritation through her. "Is that so?"

"Indeed." He leaned casually against a wooden beam, his stance that of a man thoroughly entertained.

Emma exhaled sharply and returned to her work, though she could feel his gaze lingering upon her. The weight of it was an irritation she refused to acknowledge.

She needed to focus. She needed to prove she could handle this—

And then her boot slipped.

Before she could right herself, her foot skidded across a slick patch of straw, and in an instant, she was falling.

Her back met the sodden mess she had just been clearing, the wet straw pressing against her gown, the chill of it shocking her to stillness.

For a long moment, she simply lay there, staring at the rafters above her in stunned disbelief.

Then—laughter.

A deep, unrestrained chuckle, one that carried across the stable with the kind of rich amusement that left no doubt as to its origin.

Emma blinked, shocked anew.

She turned her head slightly, only to find Lucas Wycliffe standing over her, his blue eyes glinting with mirth.

A quiet, unmistakable chuckle escaped him. It was not cruel, nor entirely unkind, but it stung nonetheless.

Emma narrowed her eyes. "You take pleasure in this, sir?"

Lucas cleared his throat, poorly disguising his grin. "I do, yes."

Emma's lips parted in outrage. "You are insufferable."

Lucas smirked, utterly unrepentant. "I did caution you

that stable work is rarely glamorous."

Emma braced herself on her elbows, her pride smarting more than her person. "You might have warned me about the wet patch."

Lucas tilted his head slightly, considering. "Where would the amusement be in that?"

Oh, he was impossible.

Impossible, and entirely too handsome for his own good.

Emma clenched her jaw, reaching up toward him without thinking.

Lucas extended a hand, his smirk lingering.

The moment their fingers met, a warmth shot through her, surprising her so thoroughly that she almost let go. His grip was firm, steady.

But before she could fully regain her footing, he pulled.

Too hard.

She stumbled slightly, the proximity between them suddenly far too close.

Lucas's hand settled instinctively at her waist, steadying her. The movement was brief, but his touch lingered.

Emma's breath caught, just for a moment.

Lucas's smirk had faded now, his blue eyes searching hers, as if he too had noticed the unspoken charge that passed between them.

Then, as quickly as it had come, the moment was gone.

Lucas stepped back, his expression reverting to that insufferable amusement once more.

"Are you injured?" he asked, though his tone held more humor than concern.

Emma straightened her posture, brushing damp straw from her gown. "Only my dignity."

Lucas grinned slyly. "That, Miss Ainsworth, is a perilous thing to bring into a stable."

She leveled him with a glare, though it held little real heat. "Do I pass your test, then?"

Lucas regarded her for a long moment, his expression unreadable.

Then, to her surprise, he nodded.

"You did not quit. That is something."

Emma fought back a smirk of her own, satisfaction flickering in her chest despite the fact that she was damp, sore, and thoroughly coated in stable filth. "I told you—I do not frighten easily."

Lucas's lips twitched, as though he were fighting another smirk.

"We shall see about that."

Emma was uncertain if that was a challenge or a warning.

Either way, she had the distinct impression that working with Lucas Wycliffe was going to prove far more complicated than she had anticipated.

She brushed a stray piece of straw from her sleeve, already thinking about the following day.

Lucas had granted her a small victory today—but she had no intention of stopping there.

She would prove to him that she was not merely another city-bred observer passing through.

And perhaps—just perhaps—she would come to understand what it was about Lucas Wycliffe that intrigued her so.

Chapter Three

The morning air held a crispness that spoke of early autumn, carrying with it the mingled scents of fresh hay, damp earth, and the unmistakable musk of horses. Emma Ainsworth had never considered herself a woman overly fond of country mornings, yet as she stood outside the grand stables of Hawthorne Manor, she had to admit there was a certain charm to the golden haze of dawn stretching over the rolling fields.

Not that she had the luxury of admiring it.

For Lucas Wycliffe was regarding her with an expression of thinly veiled impatience, as though she had already proven herself a hopeless case.

"You are late."

Emma blinked. "It is half past five in the morning."

Lucas's mouth tightened. "Dawn." He gestured toward

the horizon, where the sun had barely begun to crest the hills. "I instructed you to be here at dawn."

Emma clenched her jaw, resisting the urge to roll her eyes like a schoolgirl. "I was not aware we were running a military operation."

Lucas lifted a single brow, unimpressed. "We are running a stable. It is rather the same thing."

Emma bit back a groan, adjusting her gloves with deliberate precision. She had barely stolen four hours of sleep, her mind restless with thoughts of why she had agreed to this ridiculous arrangement in the first place.

Lucas, however, appeared entirely untroubled, standing there with all the ease of a man who found amusement in her discomfort.

"Well then," she said, folding her arms across her chest. "What do you require of me first, Sergeant?"

For a moment, his lips threatened to curve into something resembling a smirk. But instead of answering, he turned on his heel and strode toward the stable doors, motioning for her to follow.

"Come along, Miss Ainsworth. If you wish to prove your worth, you had best keep up."

Emma exhaled sharply and followed him inside, already suspecting that keeping up with Lucas Wycliffe would be no small feat.

❦

The air within the stable was cooler, the scent of hay and horses stronger beneath the shadowed beams overhead.

Lucas led her to a well-kept stall, where a chestnut mare stood quietly, her great dark eyes tracking their approach.

"This is Daisy," he said, running a hand down the horse's velvety muzzle. "She is one of our rescues. She arrived here terrified of people, but she is learning to trust again."

Emma hesitated. She had seen horses before, of course—at the occasional countryside gathering, in the parks where wealthy gentlemen paraded their fine stallions—but never up close, never like this.

She extended a hand, palm open as she had seen done in illustrations, yet before she could so much as make contact, Daisy huffed sharply and took a step back.

Emma withdrew instantly. "Well. That is rather disappointing."

Lucas chuckled, his voice rich with poorly concealed amusement. "You came on too strong."

Emma arched a brow. "I was literally standing here."

Lucas smirked, reaching for a brush from a nearby rack and handing it to her. "Horses are perceptive creatures, Miss Ainsworth. You are tense, and she knows it. Try again."

Failure wasn't an option—not now, not after her editor's sharp warnings. Every hay bale lifted, every ounce of exhaustion clawing at her limbs was a reminder of what was at stake. If she couldn't prove herself here, she would return to London with nothing more than humiliation and regret.

Emma pressed her lips together, determined now not to be bested by a horse. Taking a slow breath, she reached forward with deliberate care.

This time, Daisy's ears flicked back toward her—not entirely at ease, but not retreating either.

Lucas gave a slow nod of approval. "Better."

Emma pressed the brush lightly against the mare's side, moving in long, steady strokes as instructed. There was a soothing rhythm to it, the soft puffs of dust lifting from Daisy's coat as the bristles passed through.

It was… oddly calming.

"I shall admit," she murmured, "this is not entirely unpleasant."

Lucas gave a slow nod, the barest hint of a smile lingering. "Told you. It is not all dirt and toil."

Emma smirked. "Just mostly?"

"Precisely."

She shook her head, but despite herself, she found their banter unexpectedly easy.

At least, until Lucas said, "And what, precisely, is your true reason for being here?"

Emma froze mid-brush.

She composed herself quickly, keeping her expression neutral. "Whatever do you mean?"

Lucas leaned against the stall door, arms crossed over

his chest in that infuriatingly knowing manner. "You don't strike me as a woman content with countryside gossip. So why this particular story?"

His voice carried something softer than mockery this time—an unspoken curiosity, as though unraveling her reasons mattered more than he cared to admit.

Emma's breath hitched, not from the sharpness of the question, but from the unsettling truth that lay beneath it. He was no fool. And worse, he was genuinely interested in her answer.

Her grip on the brush tightened. She had expected resistance from him, but not this direct of a question—not so soon.

"I have already told you. I believe the work you do here is important."

Lucas studied her closely, those piercing blue eyes unreadable. "And you just so happened to find yourself in Somerset?"

Emma squared her shoulders. "My father suffered an ailment. I returned home to care for him."

A flicker of something—recognition, perhaps even understanding—crossed Lucas's face.

"That is difficult," he said, his voice quieter now.

Emma shrugged, not wanting to dwell on the emotions that stirred at the thought of her father's illness. "He is recovering. That is all that matters."

Lucas nodded slowly, though he did not seem entirely convinced.

"And once he has recovered?" He held her gaze. "You return to London?"

Emma hesitated.

She wanted to say yes.

That had been the plan, had it not?

But standing here, in this barn, brushing a mare that had once been afraid of people, speaking to a man who saw through her defenses far too easily—she was no longer certain.

"I do not know," she admitted.

Lucas did not look away. "Is that why you push so hard for this interview? Something to occupy you while you wait for an answer?"

Emma bristled. She did not like how effortlessly he seemed to read her.

She placed the brush down and straightened her posture. "I push for this interview because it is a fine story."

Lucas held her gaze for a long moment. Then, to her surprise, he gave a slow nod—as if tucking her answer away for further analysis.

"Very well." His tone was lighter now. "Then let us see if you truly intend to work for it."

❦

By midmorning, Emma Ainsworth had reached several unfortunate conclusions:

1. Grooming three horses required far more effort than she had anticipated.

2. Carrying hay bales across the stable was an unholy form of punishment.

3. Fences, though seemingly harmless, were treacherous obstacles when one was unaccustomed to them.

4. A full bucket of feed was significantly heavier than it appeared.

And the most vexing realization of all?

Lucas Wycliffe observed every one of her struggles with infuriating calmness.

She had expected sarcasm, perhaps even outright mockery. Yet, he simply assigned her another task each time, watching her as though she were some curious experiment, waiting to see if she would surrender.

By the time midday arrived, Emma was coated in dust and sweat, her limbs aching, her patience fraying at the edges.

She straightened, brushing damp tendrils from her forehead, and turned toward Lucas, who leaned against the barn door with the ease of a man wholly unaffected by the morning's exertions.

"You are enjoying this." She narrowed her gaze.

Lucas, utterly unconcerned, shrugged. "I enjoy seeing people work hard."

Emma let out an exasperated breath. "You are the worst."

Lucas smirked. "And yet, you remain."

She opened her mouth to retort, but before she could

form a suitable response, a voice rang out from the manor.

"Lucas! Are you coming for the midday meal?"

Emma turned, spotting a woman standing upon the stone steps leading to the house. She was perhaps in her early fifties, her salt-and-pepper hair neatly pinned beneath a simple cap, her expression warm yet authoritative.

Lucas nodded, pushing off from the barn wall. "In a moment, Aunt Margaret."

Emma watched as the older woman gave a knowing look before turning back toward the house.

She raised a brow. "Your aunt?"

Lucas inclined his head. "She oversees the kitchen. Ensures the men do not perish from starvation."

Emma barely suppressed a groan as her stomach—the traitor—chose that precise moment to voice its discontent.

Lucas chuckled, his blue eyes gleaming with amusement. "Well then, Miss Ainsworth, come along. You have earned your meal."

Emma let out a sigh of relief. "For once, you have said something agreeable."

Lucas merely shook his head, his expression almost... lighter.

As they walked toward the house, Emma could not quite shake the sensation that something between them had shifted.

She did not know what it meant.

But she had the distinct feeling that Lucas Wycliffe would prove a far greater challenge than she had ever anticipated.

The dining hall of Hawthorne Manor was a modest but well-kept space, its heavy oak table polished to a sheen, the scent of fresh-baked bread and roasted meats drifting enticingly through the air. The high stone fireplace, though unlit in the late summer warmth, still bore the marks of frequent use, its blackened interior a testament to the long winters endured in this part of the country.

Emma sank into one of the wooden chairs with as much grace as she could manage, her body protesting every movement. Her arms ached from carrying feed sacks, her legs from trudging across uneven ground, and her pride from her humiliating entanglement with the fence earlier that morning.

Lucas, in contrast, sat beside her with his usual ease, reaching for a pitcher of water with the fluidity of a man who had done a full morning's work and still felt entirely at ease.

Infuriating.

Aunt Margaret, standing at the head of the table, placed a large serving platter down with practiced efficiency. "You look as though you've been properly put through your paces, Miss Ainsworth."

Emma straightened, summoning what little dignity

she had left. "I am managing well enough, I believe."

Margaret's lips twitched in amusement. "Is that so?" She turned to Lucas, arching a brow. "And what is your assessment, nephew?"

Lucas, mid-slice of bread, paused only briefly before glancing toward Emma. "She hasn't quit yet."

Emma set down her fork with a bit more force than necessary. "You say that as though you expected me to."

Lucas met her gaze evenly. "I did."

Emma huffed, reaching for the bread before him and snatching the last slice from his grasp before he could take it himself.

Lucas's brows lifted slightly. "Bold move," he murmured, though the faintest twitch of amusement betrayed the fact that he had let her take it.

Emma narrowed her gaze, uncertain whether to believe she had bested him—or if, somehow, he had allowed it. Either way, she refused to give him the satisfaction of hesitation.

Emma took a deliberate bite, chewing slowly. "I shall consider it my small victory."

Margaret laughed softly, shaking her head as she ladled stew into each of their bowls. "Lord help the both of you. I've not seen a pair so determined to outmatch one another in years."

Lucas smirked. "You assume she stands a chance."

Emma lifted her spoon pointedly. "I assume nothing,

Mr. Wycliffe. I simply prove my capability."

Lucas exhaled through his nose, shaking his head but not refuting her.

Margaret, ever observant, simply smiled and turned her attention to the meal.

❧

For all the verbal sparring, the meal itself was surprisingly pleasant.

The food was far better than she had expected—warm, hearty, satisfying. Emma hadn't realized just how hungry she had become until she had finished nearly half her plate in silence, the exhaustion of the morning momentarily soothed by the simple pleasure of good food.

Across from her, Lucas was equally quiet, eating with the efficiency of a man accustomed to taking his meals quickly and without much thought.

Yet, the air between them felt different now.

Not easier, necessarily. But… less charged.

Lucas had spent the morning testing her, waiting for her to give up, to declare herself unsuited for the work.

She had not.

And though he had not said as much, she could see the faint shift in his expression—the grudging acknowledgment that she had, at the very least, held her own.

A victory, no matter how small.

When the meal was finished, Margaret gathered their plates, waving off Emma's offer to assist.

"The hands will be needing their meal soon enough. You'll be back to work in no time."

Emma barely suppressed a groan at the thought of more labor.

Lucas stood, stretching slightly, his shirt sleeves still rolled up, the morning's dust still clinging to his arms. "Come along, Ainsworth."

Emma eyed him warily. "Back to the stables already?"

Lucas tipped his head toward the back entrance. "You've earned a short reprieve. I'll show you the fields."

Emma hesitated. It was not quite an offer of peace, but it was certainly an invitation.

She took a breath, then stood. "Very well, then. Lead on."

❦

The fields behind the manor stretched for miles, rolling hills of green and gold swaying gently beneath the soft afternoon breeze. The sky was a vast, uninterrupted expanse of blue, the kind of view that stole one's breath before they even realized it.

Emma had never particularly yearned for the countryside, but standing here, with the land stretching endlessly before her, she felt an unfamiliar stirring in her chest.

Peace.

Lucas leaned against a wooden fence, arms crossed over his chest, watching her reaction with quiet amusement.

"Worth all the labor?" he asked.

Emma exhaled, glancing sideways at him. "You ask as though I have already conceded."

Lucas smirked. "You haven't?"

Emma turned back toward the fields, the wind lifting stray strands of her hair. "Not yet."

Lucas nodded once, as if satisfied with that answer.

They stood in companionable silence for a moment longer.

And though neither of them said it, something had changed between them.

Not a truce.

Not yet.

But the beginning of something neither of them had quite expected.

Chapter Four

The afternoon sun hung high over Hawthorne Manor's vast estate, casting golden light across the rolling pastures. The air had grown thick with summer heat, the kind that settled into the land, slowing movement, stretching time.

Emma Ainsworth had been on her feet since before dawn, and her body was beginning to protest in ways she had not anticipated. She had believed herself reasonably fit, accustomed to the bustling demands of city life—racing through cobblestone streets, chasing down officials for interviews, balancing the rigorous demands of her profession.

But estate work was an entirely different form of endurance.

By midafternoon, her muscles ached, a fine layer of dust clung to her dress, and the damp heat had worked its way into every seam of her clothing.

And Lucas Wycliffe?

Utterly unaffected, of course.

While she strained beneath the weight of her labor, Lucas moved with an ease so natural it seemed effortless, as if the land itself recognized him as its own. He did not pause to wipe the sweat from his brow. He did not complain. He simply worked, his actions fluid, deliberate, his every movement a testament to a lifetime spent on this land.

Emma hated to admit it, but it was… impressive.

Infuriatingly impressive.

She exhaled, brushing an errant strand of hair from her face, and turned toward the training paddock, where Lucas stood beside a young stable apprentice—a boy of no more than sixteen, his build thin, his posture uncertain.

Something about the scene made Emma pause mid-step.

She had seen Lucas be curt. Dismissive. Guarded as a fortress.

But this?

This was something else entirely.

Emma slowed her approach, pretending to be preoccupied as she lingered near the paddock fence, her hands idly dusting off the folds of her skirt as she listened.

The boy—Caleb, she recalled hearing his name earlier—stood stiffly before a striking black gelding, his fingers twitching at his sides, uncertainty written in every line of his posture.

"I—I do not believe he likes me," Caleb murmured.

Lucas crossed his arms over his chest, his expression unreadable. "He does not know you yet."

Caleb shifted uncomfortably, his boot scuffing the dirt beneath him. "Yes, but… what if I make a mistake?"

Lucas let the question settle between them for a moment, then said, "You probably will."

Caleb's head snapped up, his expression one of pure alarm.

Lucas didn't soften, but his voice shifted—lower, steadier, carrying the weight of experience rather than judgment. "Mistakes are inevitable. What matters is whether you show up again."

Caleb's brows drew together, his hands clenching at his sides.

"If you retreat at every failure," Lucas continued, "you'll never earn his trust."Caleb remained silent, the weight of those words settling heavily upon him.

Then, after a long moment, Lucas's voice dropped just slightly, almost imperceptibly softer.

"Horses do not expect perfection." His gaze did not waver. "They expect consistency. They expect you to show up. To be patient. To prove you are not going anywhere."

Emma held her breath as Caleb tentatively extended

his hand, his palm hovering just inches from the gelding's nose.

The horse flared its nostrils, considering.

Then, ever so slightly, it stepped forward, pressing its muzzle against Caleb's waiting hand.

The boy's entire face transformed.

Lucas gave a single nod, barely a smile, but something close to it. "Good."

And in that moment, something within Emma's chest shifted.

She thought of her father—how frail he had looked in his convalescence, the hollow fear in his eyes when he had believed himself forgotten. There had been days when she felt helpless to offer comfort, powerless to ease his fear. But watching Caleb now—watching Lucas encourage belief where there had once been none—she realized that sometimes, the smallest acts of patience could offer the greatest hope.

She had spent two days attempting to untangle Lucas Wycliffe, trying to determine whether he was simply another brooding countryman with a hardened exterior and a past he refused to acknowledge.

But watching him now, she saw something else entirely.

This was not cold indifference.

This was a man who cared far more than he allowed anyone to see.

Lucas must have sensed her watching.

The very moment Caleb led the gelding away, his steps lighter, his confidence subtly restored, Lucas turned toward her.

Emma did not look away.

"You are good at that." She nodded toward where Caleb had been standing only moments before.

Lucas raised a single brow. "At what, precisely?"

She tilted her head slightly. "Instilling belief. Encouraging others to see themselves as capable."

Lucas was silent for a long moment, his expression unreadable. Then, with a nonchalant shrug, he murmured, "The boy merely needs someone to believe in him first."

Something about the way he said it made Emma's stomach tighten.

She had seen that same doubt before—in children left to fend for themselves in the crowded streets of London, in young boys who had been dismissed by the very people meant to protect them, in men and women who had been overlooked before they ever had a chance.

She studied Lucas, wondering—for the first time—if he had ever felt that way himself.

She was not sure why, but the thought stirred something deep inside her.

"Why do you do it?" she asked, shifting slightly so she could face him fully. "The estate, the rescues, the boys who come to work here?"

Lucas did not answer right away.

Instead, he leaned against the wooden fence, his gaze drifting toward the horizon, as though the answer lay somewhere in the open fields before him.

Emma did not rush him.

She simply waited.

Finally, Lucas exhaled, the sound quiet but deliberate.

"Because it matters."

That was it. No long-winded speech. No dramatic monologue.

Just a simple, quiet truth.

And somehow, that made it even more powerful.

❦

The sun had begun its slow descent, casting long golden streaks of light through the wooden slats of the stable walls.The air had cooled slightly, the oppressive heat of midday giving way to the softer embrace of evening.

Emma found herself once more within the main barn, assisting Lucas in storing the riding tack from the day's lessons.

She was exhausted, sore in muscles she hadn't known existed, and acutely aware that she was in desperate need of a bath.

And yet—

There was something oddly satisfying about the work.

The simple, methodical nature of it. The quiet rhythm of labor that required no debate, no argument, no scrutiny.

For a while, they worked in companionable silence, the only sounds the soft creak of leather, the distant calls of horses in the pasture, the occasional rustling of hay beneath their boots.

Then—

"I meant what I said earlier."

Lucas glanced at her. "About what?"

Emma carefully placed a bridle upon its hook, smoothing the worn leather with her fingertips.

"You are good at what you do."

She hesitated briefly before continuing.

"This place… these boys… they are fortunate to have you."

She had not meant for the words to sound so… earnest.

But they were true.

Lucas stilled.

Something flickered in his expression—brief, fleeting. Something deeply buried. For the first time since meeting him, she thought she caught a glimpse of genuine vulnerability—an old hurt, perhaps, woven into the fabric of the man before her.

For a single, breathless moment, she thought he might actually respond.

Then—

"I should finish in the back."

The words were quiet but firm.

And then he turned away.

Emma felt the loss of his attention like the sudden slam of a door.

She exhaled, shaking her head slightly. "Right. Of course."

Lucas hesitated for just a fraction of a second, his fingers tightening around the leather reins he held.

Then—without another word—he was gone.

That night, Emma lay in bed, staring up at the canopy of her childhood chamber, her thoughts a tangled, restless mess.

She had returned to the village of Dunster believing she would remain only for a matter of weeks. Just long enough to tend to her father, complete her article, and then return to London.

But now?

Now, she was not so certain.

Lucas Wycliffe was not an easy man to know.

He was closed-off, stubborn as an ox, and made it painfully clear that he had no interest in offering explanations for his guarded nature.

And yet—

Today had revealed something else entirely.

She had seen a man who cared—even if he veiled that care beneath layers of indifference.

A man who believed in second chances, not merely for those in need but for the creatures under his care.

A man who—despite his best efforts—was beginning to make her question everything she thought she wanted.

And that?

That was a problem.

A very dangerous problem.

Because Emma had spent her entire career learning how to keep herself detached, to observe without entanglement.

And yet, Lucas Wycliffe was precisely the sort of man a woman could become dangerously entangled with.

The man who remained a mystery even as his kindness revealed itself in fleeting moments. A man who seemed determined to hold the world at arm's length—perhaps because he feared what might happen if someone truly stayed.

And that?

That was the last thing she needed.

❦

Chapter Five

The following morning, Emma Ainsworth woke with an ache in muscles she had not previously known existed.

The demands of estate life had proven far more rigorous than she had anticipated, and her body resented her for it. Yet, no matter the soreness in her limbs, she had resolved that she would not let Lucas Wycliffe know.

By the time she arrived at the stable yard, he was already there—of course, he was.

He stood by the corral, speaking in low, measured tones to one of the stable hands as he secured the saddle upon a chestnut mare.

There was a certain effortless grace to his movements, as if even the most laborious of tasks came to him with remarkable ease. It was, Emma noted with great irritation, one of the many aspects of his existence that made him entirely insufferable.

She approached, arms folded primly. "You know, I am beginning to suspect you take great pleasure in my suffering."

Lucas lifted his gaze, his mouth twitching at the corners. "Beginning to?"

Emma let out a dramatic sigh. "Simply give me today's task list, so that I may steel myself for whatever fresh torment you have devised."

Lucas adjusted the girth strap, patting the mare's flank before turning to her. "Good news."

Emma arched a brow. "Somehow, I doubt that."

"No mucking of stalls today."

She blinked, momentarily at a loss. "You are serious?"

Lucas smirked. "Entirely."

Emma eyed him suspiciously. "And what, pray, is the alternative?"

Lucas finished securing the saddle before resting a hand on the mare's neck, his expression untroubled, as if this were merely another unremarkable morning.

"Today, you are assisting with preparations for the Fayre."

Emma frowned. "Fayre?"

Lucas regarded her with thinly veiled disbelief, as if she had just declared the sky to be purple. "The Harvest Fayre. A grand occasion. Happens every autumn. Do not tell me you have forgotten."

Emma had not forgotten.

Not exactly.

She had merely… not given it much thought.

In her youth, the Autumn Harvest Fayre had been one of the finest spectacles of the season—filled with hayrides, cider tastings, a village-wide baking competition, and, of course, the infamous Fayre Dance.

But it had been years since she had attended.

For the past decade, she had been too preoccupied with her career, too entangled in the bustle of London, to think of quaint country traditions.

She hesitated before finally saying, "I did not forget. I simply did not think it was still… relevant."

Lucas's brows lifted. "You cannot be serious."

Emma shrugged. "What, is it still the same old festivities? A bit of cider and a handful of poorly choreographed country reels?"

Lucas shook his head slowly, his expression one of pure amusement. "City girl, you have no idea what you are in for."

❧

As it turned out, preparing for the Autumn Harvest Fayre was nothing short of a grand production.

Emma spent the better part of the morning hauling bundles of hay, assisting in the hanging of lanterns along the village square, and arranging long wooden tables beneath a grand pavilion, where the evening's celebratory feast would be held.

It was noisy, chaotic, entirely unorganized…

And, to her great surprise, rather enjoyable.

She had forgotten how closely knit the village of Dunster truly was—how each person contributed their time and effort, ensuring that the event came together in a way that felt almost… magical.

As Emma hung the lanterns, her fingers grazed the rough twine—an oddly familiar sensation. The scent of spiced cider in the air transported her back to another fayre long ago, her father's warm hand steadying her as they weaved through the crowded square, laughter echoing from children dashing between hay bales. She had been just a girl then, clutching a caramel apple, the glow of lanterns painting the night sky in soft amber hues.

Everywhere she turned, a familiar face greeted her as if she had never left. For the first time in years, the memory didn't feel distant—it felt like coming home.

Mrs. Whitmore, the kindly baker's wife, pulled her into a warm embrace, recalling aloud how Emma had once snuck sweets from her shop as a child.

Mr. Evans, the widowed blacksmith, clapped her on the shoulder, his smile kind and knowing. "Good to see you back, Miss Ainsworth. Feels like old times, don't it?"

She had not expected it—the sense of belonging that settled in her chest.

As she moved through the square, Emma's steps

slowed before the old fountain—its stone edges worn smooth by years of passing hands and laughter. A memory surfaced unbidden: her younger self, gripping her father's hand, her laughter ringing out as they watched the autumn leaves swirl into the water.

"You'll make a wish for the future, won't you, darling?" her father had asked, voice warm with affection.

Now, standing in that same square, surrounded by familiar faces and the scent of cider and spiced apples, Emma felt that same wish stir within her—a longing not just for success, but for something deeper. Something like home.

For the first time in a very long time, Emma did not feel like an outsider.

❦

By midday, the village square had transformed. Wreaths of golden leaves adorned the shopfronts, and long ribbons of deep red and orange wove between the lantern poles, creating a breathtaking display of autumnal beauty.

The scent of spiced cider, warm cinnamon, and crisp apples filled the air, blending with the rich, earthen aroma of hay bales stacked neatly around the seating areas.

Emma paused to wipe a sheen of perspiration from her brow, glancing around to take in their handiwork.

"Not bad," a voice drawled beside her.

She turned, finding Lucas standing not far from where she stood, his arms crossed over his chest, his gaze sweeping over the fayre preparations with quiet approval.

Emma smirked. "Careful, Mr. Wycliffe. That almost sounded like a compliment."

Lucas's lips twitched slightly, but he said nothing at first.

Then—too casually, far too casually—he spoke.

"You planning to attend the dance tomorrow?"

Emma blinked. "The dance?"

"Yes. You know, the grand event that takes place every single year?"

Emma shifted slightly. She had not truly considered it.

The Fayre Dance had once been the highlight of her autumn season. She could still remember the lanterns glowing against the night sky, the sound of lively strings filling the air, the way the entire village gathered for an evening of revelry and merriment.

But… it had been years.

She hesitated. "I don't know. I have not given it much thought."

Lucas studied her for a long moment. Then, with deliberate ease, he said,

"You should go," Lucas said, voice low and steady, yet there was a softness beneath the words—barely there, but unmistakable. His gaze didn't linger, fixed instead on the horizon as though the invitation wasn't truly for the fayre at all, but something quieter, unspoken.

Something about the way he said it made her pulse

falter for a fraction of a second. Emma wasn't sure if he was suggesting the fayre was for her benefit—or his own.

She crossed her arms. "Are you going?"

His mouth curved just slightly, that infuriating half-smile making its appearance. "Perhaps."

Emma narrowed her eyes. "You do not seem the sort to engage in formal dancing."

"I don't."

Lucas's answer was immediate.

Then—after a pause—he added, "But I might make an exception."

Emma's stomach did a most ridiculous thing—a tiny, fluttering sensation she was certain must be the result of exhaustion rather than… anything else.

Was he… flirting?

No. Surely not.

Lucas Wycliffe did not flirt.

Lucas Wycliffe barely spoke in full sentences.

And yet… there was something in his expression, something unreadable, something almost teasing—almost inviting—that unsettled her in a way she was not entirely prepared for.

"Are you asking me to attend with you?" she inquired, arching a brow.

Lucas chuckled, shaking his head. "I'm only saying… you should be there."

Emma studied him carefully, attempting to discern the

meaning beneath his words.

Lucas Wycliffe was not an easy man to interpret.

But something told her this was as close to an invitation as she would ever receive.

And, for some unfathomable reason…

That made her want to say yes.

The day had drawn to a close, and with it, the bustling energy of fayre preparations had faded into a quiet hum of anticipation for the festivities to come. The lanterns strung across the village square flickered softly in the approaching dusk, casting warm golden light upon the cobbled streets.

Yet, despite the liveliness of the village, Emma found herself wandering away from the crowd, her steps carrying her toward the corral.

She leaned against the wooden fence, her gaze sweeping across the vast pastureland as the sun melted into the horizon.

The sky was a masterpiece of deep amber and dusky violet, the kind of breathtaking countryside view she had forgotten she loved.

The stillness of it settled something inside her—something she had not realized was restless.

Footsteps sounded behind her, steady and familiar.

Lucas.

He came to stand beside her, silent for a long moment,

his arms braced against the top rail of the fence.

Then, in that quiet, contemplative voice of his, he asked, "You thinking about London?"

Emma turned her head slightly, surprised by the question. "What makes you think that?"

Lucas shrugged, his gaze never leaving the horizon. "You have that look."

Emma arched a brow. "What look?"

Lucas's jaw tightened ever so slightly, his gaze drifting out toward the fields.

"Because I know the look of someone wondering if they belong somewhere else." His voice was quiet now, heavy with unspoken memory. "I used to think about leaving, too."

Emma turned toward him, surprised by the admission. "You did?"

He nodded slowly. "There was a time when this place felt… suffocating. Like every inch of it reminded me of things I couldn't change." His fingers flexed against the wooden fence. "But running wouldn't have fixed anything."

The raw honesty in his voice made her chest tighten. Perhaps Lucas Wycliffe wasn't just a man of solitude— but someone who had chosen to stay and carry the weight of his past.

Her heart skipped a beat.

Because… he wasn't wrong.

For so long, she had thought of Dunster as nothing more than a temporary waypoint, a place she had outgrown long ago.

But now, standing here… surrounded by familiar faces, familiar places, the easy rhythm of a life she had left behind… she wasn't sure of anything anymore.

She swallowed, turning her attention back to the fading light.

"And what about you?" she asked, her voice quieter now.

Lucas did not answer at once.

Instead, he exhaled, his gaze still fixed on the rolling fields before them.

Lucas shifted slightly, arms folding across the top of the fence. "This place has a way of keeping you longer than you mean to."

His voice carried the weight of experience—of a man who had not just stayed out of duty, but perhaps because the world beyond these fields had offered nothing worth leaving for.

Emma turned toward him, something softening inside her. "Perhaps that isn't always a bad thing."

There was something final in his tone, something resolute.

Emma envied that.

She had never felt that way about any place before.

Never felt rooted. Never felt like she truly belonged anywhere.

And yet, standing here beside Lucas Wycliffe, she wondered if perhaps—just perhaps—she had never truly allowed herself the chance.

Lucas turned to her then, his expression unreadable, his voice steady.

"You coming to the dance or not?"

Emma felt a slow smile tug at her lips.

"I suppose you'll just have to wait and see."

Lucas chuckled, shaking his head as though he had expected no less. "Figured as much."

And then—without another word—he turned and strode away, disappearing into the dimming twilight.

Emma watched him go, feeling more questions than answers settling in her chest.

Because for the first time in a long time…

She wasn't entirely certain where she was meant to be.

Chapter Six

The Autumn Harvest Fayre was in full revelry, and to her great surprise, Emma Ainsworth had to admit—it was rather enchanting.

The village square was alive with laughter and music, the air thick with the scent of mulled wine, roasted chestnuts, and warm spice cakes. Strings of paper lanterns and garlands of autumn leaves crisscrossed above, bathing the scene in a soft, golden glow.

Merchants lined the streets, displaying their finest wares—handwoven shawls, polished wooden trinkets, and delicate lacework. Bakers sold freshly made tarts, their sugared surfaces glistening in the lantern light, while children darted between hay bales, their delighted shrieks echoing through the night.

It was precisely the sort of event she had once taken for granted—before she had packed her life into a single trunk and departed for London, certain she was meant for something grander.

And yet—

As she moved through the throng of revelers, dodging dancing couples and laughing villagers, Emma felt something stir within her.

A sense of belonging. A sense of nostalgia she had not anticipated.

Her gaze caught a glimpse of the old lantern-maker's stall, where delicate glass bulbs shimmered under the flickering light. She remembered visiting that very spot as a child, her fingers sticky with apple tart as her father lifted her onto his shoulders so she could hang a lantern of her own. A wave of bittersweet nostalgia washed over her—this fayre wasn't just a village tradition; it was a thread of her past, woven into the very fabric of Dunster.

And yet, something was missing.

Or rather—someone.

Lucas Wycliffe was nowhere to be found.

She should have expected as much.

Lucas was not the sort to waltz beneath the lanterns or indulge in idle chatter over spiced cider. He was a man of quiet resolve, one who preferred the open fields, the stillness of the countryside, the quiet presence of his horses over the company of people.

Which meant, by all reason, she should cease looking for him.

And yet—

She caught herself scanning the crowd once more, searching for a familiar, broad-shouldered figure.

Emma inhaled sharply, chiding herself.

This was foolishness.

And yet, despite her best efforts, she could not deny the flicker of disappointment.

Damn it.

Emma had nearly resigned herself to leaving when she finally spotted him.

At the very edge of the fayre grounds, away from the music and laughter, stood Lucas Wycliffe.

He was leaning against a wooden fence, his hands tucked into the pockets of his coat, his gaze fixed upon the great bonfire that roared before him.

The flames cast flickering shadows across his features, illuminating the sharp angles of his face, the way his brow creased slightly in thought.

He looked as though the fire held secrets only he could hear.

Emma hesitated.

She could turn away.

Or—

She could walk toward him and see what happened.

The choice was made before she had time to think.

"I did not take you for the fayre-going sort."

Lucas turned his head slightly, his expression unreadable as the firelight danced in his blue eyes. "I did not take you for someone who would remain in Dunster this long."

Emma smirked, settling beside him against the fence. "Surprised?"

Lucas's mouth twitched at the corners, just slightly. "A little."

Silence settled between them—but it was not an uncomfortable one.

The fire crackled and hissed, sending golden embers drifting into the night air. The cool autumn breeze carried the distant sound of fiddles and laughter from the village square, but here, at the edge of the fayre, it felt… quieter.

For the first time since she had returned, Emma felt still.

Settled.

And perhaps—

Perhaps that was dangerous.

Because settling was not something she had ever been particularly good at.

Emma let the quiet linger between them, the distant hum of laughter and music from the fayre fading beneath the snap and crackle of the fire. The warmth of the flames flickered over Lucas's features, illuminating the sharp angles of his face, the quiet intensity of his gaze as he stared into the embers.

She tilted her head, studying him.

"Tell me something."

Lucas glanced at her, his brows lifting slightly. "What?"

"Why do you always stand on the edge of things?"

His expression did not change, but she caught the barest flicker of something in his eyes.

"You never stand in the middle of the action," she continued, gesturing toward the fayre behind them. "You are always here. Watching, but never participating."

Lucas exhaled, rubbing the back of his neck. "Never been much for crowds."

"That is not it."

He turned his head slightly, as if surprised by her insistence.

"You keep people at a distance," she observed.

For the first time that evening, his jaw tightened—just slightly—but enough that she noticed.

Emma watched him carefully. "I think you like being on the outside." She hesitated, then added, "Less chance of getting hurt that way."

Lucas said nothing at first.

Then, in a voice softer than she expected, he murmured, "Or maybe I just don't belong in the middle."

Emma felt something tighten in her chest.

Because she knew that feeling all too well.

And she wasn't sure which was more unsettling—that she saw through Lucas Wycliffe… or that, somehow, he saw through her, too.

From the village square, the sound of a violin drifted toward them—a slow, lilting melody, the kind that called for soft steps and quiet intimacy.

Emma glanced at Lucas.

Then, without thinking, she extended a hand.

Lucas's brows furrowed. "What are you doing?"

"Dancing."

Lucas let out a low scoff. "I do not dance."

"Come now." She wiggled her fingers. "I promise not to judge you."

He hesitated.

Emma could see the wariness in his eyes, the way he glanced at her outstretched hand as if it were some dangerous thing.

Then, with an exasperated sigh, he took it.

Emma barely had time to process the warmth of his fingers entwining with hers before he pulled her in—closer than she had expected.

Her breath hitched.

The firelight flickered between them, casting dancing

shadows across his face, highlighting the depth of his steady, unreadable gaze.

They swayed, just slightly, to the music no one else could hear.

Lucas's hands were warm, solid, unyielding as they rested at her waist.

Emma's pulse skipped a beat.

This was… unexpected.

And yet, somehow, it felt inevitable.

Like a slow-burning match meeting its flame.

For a moment, Emma thought he might kiss her.

And for the first time in a long time, she wanted some-one to.

She tilted her chin up, her breath mingling with his in the cool night air.

Lucas's gaze flicked to her lips, just briefly.

Then—

"Emma."

His voice was rough, almost pained.

She swallowed. "Yes?"

Lucas exhaled, his grip tightening slightly at her waist.

Then—as if some invisible line had been crossed—he took a step back.

Emma felt the loss of warmth like a physical thing.

Damn it.

Lucas ran a hand through his hair, his fingers threading through the dark strands in a gesture of barely restrained frustration.

His gaze flickered—a war waged behind those unreadable blue eyes.

"This… probably isn't a good idea," he muttered.

Emma forced a wry smirk, though her chest ached with something she dared not name.

"The dancing?" she teased, trying for lightness.

Lucas's gaze snapped to hers, sharp and unyielding.

"You know what I mean."

Her smirk faltered.

She swallowed, hating how much those words stung.

Because for one fleeting moment, she had thought—

No.

She would not allow herself to fall into that trap.

He was right.

This was not a good idea.

So why did it feel as though she were walking away from something she might regret?

Emma turned on her heel before he could say anything else.

She needed air.

Needed space.

Her steps carried her toward the outskirts of the fayre, where the glow of the lanterns faded and the night stretched wide and open above her.

The stars—brilliant, endless, untouched by time—twinkled above the pastures, casting their silver glow upon the quiet fields.

She inhaled deeply, willing herself to let go of the lingering warmth on her skin, the phantom weight of Lucas's hand at her waist.

She should have known better.

Lucas Wycliffe was not the sort of man who let people in.

And yet…

Emma absently touched her wrist, where his fingers had rested just moments before.

Her skin was still warm.

And no matter how much she tried to push the moment away, she knew one thing with absolute certainty—

Lucas Wycliffe was a dangerous kind of man.

The kind who could make a woman forget where she was going.

Or worse—

Make her question whether she truly wanted to leave at all.

Chapter Seven

The following morning, Emma Ainsworth awoke with a singular, unshakable thought.

She needed to clear her mind.

The night before had been too close, too charged with something she was not yet prepared to name.

Lucas Wycliffe was not supposed to be someone she became entangled with.

Her return to Somersetshire was meant to be temporary—a chance to care for her father, complete her article, and prove to both herself and her editor that she still had her journalistic edge.

That was all.

So why, then, was she standing before Hawthorne Manor's grand stable, staring at Lucas Wycliffe as though he were a puzzle she was suddenly desperate to solve?

By the time she found him, Lucas was already at work.

No surprise there.

Her fingers flexed against the folds of her skirt, hesitation clawing at the edges of her resolve. Perhaps it would be wiser to leave the moment unspoken, to let the tension of the fayre night dissolve into the silence of a new day. After all, what good could come of poking at a wound barely scabbed over?

And yet… every fiber of her being rebelled against retreat. She had faced men twice as arrogant, in grander cities with far more to lose. Why, then, did this feel so much more dangerous?

Steeling herself, she stepped forward, each stride a battle against the fear of revealing too much—or discovering something she wasn't ready to face.

He stood near the paddock fence, crouched beside one of the rescue horses, inspecting its foreleg with silent concentration. His sleeves were rolled to the elbows, his strong hands moving with practiced ease, his focus entirely locked upon the task before him.

Emma hesitated.

Perhaps she ought to simply pretend the previous night had never happened.

Perhaps they could return to the playful, unspoken challenge between them—the easy banter, the quiet competition of proving herself in a world he believed she did not belong in.

She could ignore the way her pulse had skipped when he had held her close, the way he had looked at her as if he wanted to kiss her—but would not allow himself to.

Yes. That was the plan.

She would act normal. Casual. As though nothing had changed.

So, naturally, the first words out of her mouth were—

"Are you going to pretend last night never happened?"

Lucas stiffened.

Damn it.

He turned slowly, his blue eyes steady, unreadable.

"Wasn't planning on it."

Emma faltered.

"Good. Because I—" She stopped. Blinking. Wait.

"What?"

Lucas straightened, brushing the dust from his hands, then leaned casually against the fence.

"I wasn't planning on pretending."

Emma stared at him.

Well, that was unexpected.

"I…" She swallowed, suddenly thrown off balance. "Very well. So… what are we doing then?"

Lucas tilted his head slightly, his gaze settling upon her as though he were studying her reaction.

"I don't know." He paused. "What do you want us to

be doing?"

Emma's stomach twisted.

Because that was the question, wasn't it?

What did she want?

Last night had been… something.

But she was not yet certain what.

And judging by the way Lucas was watching her now, neither was he.

❧

For a long moment, neither of them spoke.

The distant sounds of the estate carried on as usual—the soft nickering of horses, the wind rustling through the trees, the distant chime of a bell from the village beyond.

His jaw tightened, and his gaze drifted toward the open fields, searching for something distant and untouchable.

Then, at last, Lucas exhaled.

"You don't understand," he murmured again—this time quieter, as though the words were meant more for himself than for her.

But when he turned back, her eyes met his with an unwavering steadiness. Not prying, not pitying—just waiting.

And somehow, that was worse than any demand she could have made.

"Fine," Lucas muttered, voice thick with reluctance. "You want your interview? You've earned it."

Emma blinked. "What?"

He crossed his arms over his broad chest, his stance unwavering. "You have been working yourself to exhaustion, and you have not yet fled. I would say you have earned it."

Emma narrowed her eyes. "What is the catch?"

Lucas's lips tugged into that infuriating almost-smile, a glimmer of amusement flickering across his otherwise unreadable features.

"No personal questions."

Lucas's jaw tightened—a muscle twitching in defiance of the calm expression he tried so desperately to maintain. His gaze darkened, fixed not on her but on some distant memory she could not see, could not name.

"No personal questions," he said again, voice rough, brittle like old wood threatening to splinter. "That's the condition."

And just for a moment, Emma saw it—the fracture in his armor, the glimpse of something deeper, something raw and aching, buried beneath years of silence.

Emma scoffed. "That is not how this works."

"It is if you want the interview."

She frowned, torn between triumph and frustration.

For the past week, she had tried to crack him open, to unravel the story behind the brooding, enigmatic horseman who had chosen to bury himself in the solitude of this place.

And now, when she was finally close—he was still keeping the walls up.

"Lucas," she started, her tone softening. "People do not simply vanish from the world overnight. One day, you were a rising equestrian champion, the next, you are a ghost. If you are willing to speak about why this land matters to you, why not tell the entire story?"

Lucas's jaw tightened.

"You would not understand."

Emma's frustration spiked.

"Try me."

Lucas turned away, running a hand through his dark hair, and for the first time since she had met him, he actually looked… unsettled.

Like he wasn't just annoyed at her persistence.

Like he was fighting something inside himself.

Emma's chest tightened.

"Lucas—"

"It is just horses," he said abruptly.

Emma stilled. "Pardon?"

He turned back to her, his expression carefully guarded, but his voice a fraction too tight.

"This estate, the boys who come here, the rescues—it is just horses, Emma. They needed a place, I provided one. That is all there is to it."

Liar.

She could hear it in his voice, see it in his posture, the way his fists clenched like he was restraining something.

He was lying.

This place—it meant something to him.

Something he was not yet ready to admit.

Emma inhaled slowly, choosing her next words carefully.

"Very well," she said at last. "No personal questions."

Lucas nodded once. "Tomorrow, then."

And just like that, he turned and strode away, leaving Emma standing there.

More determined than ever to uncover the truth.

❦

That night, Emma sat in her childhood chamber, the glow of a single candle flickering against the darkened walls.

Her journal lay open before her, pages covered in scribbled notes, but the words blurred together, her focus scattered.

Her thoughts were a mess.

She had collected details about the estate, the boys who had come through its gates, the stories of rescued horses Lucas had taken in when no one else would.

But the one thing missing?

Lucas himself.

Everything about him remained a mystery.

And she was no longer certain if it was only the journalist in her that wanted to solve it.

Because, for the first time in her career, this was not just about the story anymore.

And that?

That was dangerous.

She knew what happened when one stepped too close, when curiosity turned to something deeper.

She had learned the hard way.

And she was not sure she was ready to make that mistake again.

❦

Lucas lay awake, staring at the wooden beams of the ceiling, arms folded behind his head, listening to the quiet symphony of the estate at night.

It should have been calming.

Instead, he felt restless.

Like something had shifted inside him, and he did not know how to put it back in its place.

Emma Ainsworth was getting under his skin.

That was the problem.

He had spent years ensuring his past remained buried, keeping his distance, making certain that no one pried too deeply.

And yet, here she was—pushing, questioning, making him want to say things he had long since locked away.

And that dance?

That had been a mistake.

Because for a moment—a single, reckless moment—he had wanted more.

And he could not afford that.

Emma was not staying.

She would write her article, pack her bags, and return to London.

She had made that clear.

So why the hell did the thought of her leaving feel so damn wrong?

Lucas exhaled slowly, closing his eyes.

This was going to end badly.

He could feel it.

He squeezed his eyes shut, forcing the memory of her outstretched hand from his mind, the ghost of her touch lingering against his skin far longer than it should have.

Lucas had buried his past for a reason. Every secret, every regret—locked away where they couldn't hurt him or anyone else. Letting her in would unravel everything.

But it was already happening, wasn't it?

The walls he had spent years fortifying were beginning to crack. And in the silence of that cold, restless night, one truth echoed louder than the rest:

Emma Ainsworth was dangerous.

And he was already too close to falling.

And yet, when he thought about pulling away, creating distance—

All he could remember was the way she had felt in his arms last night.

And worse…

How much he wanted to feel it again.

❦

Chapter Eight

The following morning, Emma Ainsworth arrived at Hawthorne Manor's stables armed with her leather-bound notebook, graphite pencil, and a determination as unyielding as the morning sun.

Lucas Wycliffe had given her an inch.

She intended to take a mile.

Yet, as she approached the great timber-framed barn, she knew persuading him to relinquish even a sliver of his guarded past would be as difficult as prying open an iron vault with a hairpin.

Lucas was already at work.

No surprise there.

He stood near the feeding troughs, tossing fresh hay into the stalls with that infuriating ease as though the weight of the task did not even graze him. The rolled sleeves of his linen shirt revealed the strong, tanned forearms of a man accustomed to labor, the effortless movement of his frame betraying a natural strength that—if she were being entirely honest—ought not to be distracting.

And yet.

She exhaled sharply.

He knew precisely why she had come.

But why was she here—really?

It wasn't just the article anymore. Each glance, each unspoken word between them, chipped away at her carefully built defenses.

And that was dangerous. Because she had spent years perfecting the art of detachment—never letting anyone close enough to unravel her. Yet, Lucas Wycliffe didn't need grand gestures or elaborate speeches. His silence said enough. And every moment she spent near him… it scared her how much she wanted to stay.

And judging by the way he did not even glance in her direction, he had no intention of making this easy.

Emma's fingers tightened around her notebook.

She took a breath.

Very well. Game on.

But as she stood there, notebook in hand, a flicker of doubt gnawed at the edge of her resolve.

What was she doing? This wasn't just about the article anymore—she felt it every time Lucas looked at her with that unreadable stare, every time the walls around him seemed to close tighter.

This wasn't just about proving herself to her editor. It was about proving something to herself—that she could still see the truth behind the fortress of another person's silence. That she wasn't just running from her own failures.

❦

She leaned against the stall, flipping open her notebook with deliberate ease.

"Very well, let us proceed."

Lucas did not pause in his task.

"Proceed with what?"

"The interview. You said I had earned it."

Lucas sighed, grabbing another bundle of hay and tossing it effortlessly over the wooden partition before finally turning to face her.

"You have your interview, Miss Ainsworth. But do not expect anything remarkable."

Emma grinned slyly. "I never expect much from reluctant horsemen."

His mouth twitched—just slightly—but he did not take the bait. Instead, he motioned toward a weathered wooden bench near the stable doors.

"Fine. Let us have it over with."

Emma followed him, turning to a fresh page in her notebook, pencil poised to extract whatever slivers of truth might slip through his carefully constructed defenses.

"Very well," she began. "Tell me about Hawthorne Manor and its stables."

Lucas exhaled. "It is an estate."

Emma arched a brow. "Fascinating. Utterly riveting. Let us delve a little deeper, shall we?"

Lucas rubbed a hand over his jaw, his exasperation palpable. "We take in horses that need a second chance. Some have been mistreated, some abandoned. We rehabilitate them, give them purpose."

Something flickered in his gaze then—brief, unguarded. Something real.

Emma latched onto it.

"And what made you wish to begin such a venture?"

The moment the words left her lips, his entire posture shifted.

His jaw tightened. His shoulders squared. The warmth in his expression cooled to a carefully controlled nothingness.

"It seemed the right thing to do."

Emma did not believe him for a second.

❀

She leaned forward. "That is not an answer."

Lucas's gaze met hers—cool, unreadable.

"It is the only answer you shall receive."

Emma crossed her arms. "You are avoiding the question."

Lucas stood, towering over her now, exuding the quiet authority of a man accustomed to ending conversations at his discretion.

His eyes darkened, and for a moment, something raw flickered across his expression—a flash of memory, of pain, buried beneath years of practiced indifference.

"You don't understand," he said, voice lower, rougher. "Some stories aren't meant for sharing."

But Emma didn't back down. The quiet defiance in her stance, the way she met his gaze without fear—damn it, it made him want to trust her. And that was dangerous.

"You agreed—no personal inquiries."

"I am asking about the estate." She lifted her chin. "Surely that does not fall within the realm of personal?"

"No."

He turned back toward the stall, lifting a coil of rope from its hook, his movements slow and deliberate.

"Personal would be asking why I left competition. Or what transpired before I came here. That, Miss Ainsworth, is not part of the agreement."

Emma studied him for a long moment, frustration simmering just beneath the surface.

She tapped her pencil against her notebook. "Very well," she conceded at last, "then let us discuss why this endeavor is important to you."

Lucas hesitated.

It was brief, but she caught it.

Then, just as quickly, he shook his head.

"It simply is."

Emma clenched her jaw. "You are remarkably gifted at evasion."

Lucas's lips pressed into a thin line. "You are pushing, Miss Ainsworth."

"Because you are hiding."

His expression darkened slightly. "Or perhaps I simply do not owe you my past."

Emma's heart pounded.

For the first time since arriving, she sensed the first true crack in his armor.

And she was not about to let it go unnoticed.

❦

Emma rose abruptly from the bench, her pulse quickening, frustration simmering beneath her carefully composed exterior.

Before she could think better of it, she stepped closer, into his space—challenging, unyielding.

"I am not asking for your life story, Lucas." Her voice was steady, but there was an edge to it now, something raw, something she had not intended to reveal.

"I am asking for something real."

Lucas's jaw tightened, his entire posture stiffening as though bracing for impact.

For a brief, fleeting moment, she thought he might actually speak.

Might actually give her something more than evasion.

But then—

He stepped back.

He always did.

The air between them stretched taut, something unsaid hanging in the silence.

Lucas shook his head, his voice low, controlled, and utterly final.

"I do not do this."

Emma refused to let it drop.

"Do what?" she demanded, her breath shallow. "Talk? Allow people in? Or simply accept that perhaps—just perhaps—you are not as untouchable as you pretend to be?"

Lucas's eyes flashed.

For a single second, just one, he looked as though he might fight back.

Might tell her exactly what lay beneath his carefully constructed walls.

Then—

He exhaled sharply, his expression smoothing into something impassive, impenetrable.

"The interview is over."

And just like that, he turned on his heel and strode out of the stable, his retreating form disappearing into the crisp morning light.

But the words burned as he said them.

Every muscle in his body screamed for distance, for space—to retreat before she could get any closer.

Yet as he walked away, the memory of her eyes—steady, unflinching, almost… understanding—followed him like a shadow he couldn't shake.

Emma stood motionless, her fingers gripping her notebook so tightly it bent beneath the pressure.

She closed her eyes, inhaling deeply, forcing herself to steady the storm raging inside her.

This was no longer about the article.

This was about him.

And that realization?

That was the most dangerous one of all.

Lucas strode toward the paddock, his boots pressing into the damp earth, his breath measured but tight.

He needed distance.

He needed air.

He had let her get too close. Again.

And the worst part?

He had wanted to tell her.

He had wanted to tell her about the accident, about why he had walked away from competition, about the ghosts that followed him through every quiet moment of the night.

But if he did?

She would leave.

She would write her article, pack her belongings, and return to London.

And he…

He would still be here.

Lucas gritted his teeth, his gaze fixed upon the vast expanse of the estate.

A memory clawed its way to the surface—hooves pounding across the competition field, the sharp intake of breath just before everything went wrong. The snap of bone, the deafening silence that followed.

He had buried it deep. Tried to forget the shame, the loss, the guilt that followed him like a shadow.

And now, she was digging it up—without even meaning to.

This was why he never allowed people in.

Because when they left, they always took a piece of him with them.

And Lucas Wycliffe was done losing pieces of himself.

❦

Emma sat in her father's carriage, gripping the reins tightly, her pulse unsteady, her gaze locked on the wide-open land stretching beyond Hawthorne Manor's sprawling estate.

She had come here expecting a simple human-interest piece—one that would reestablish her credibility as a journalist.

Instead, she was staring at a story she was no longer

certain she knew how to write.

Lucas Wycliffe was more than a reclusive horseman with a past.

He was wounded, guarded, impossibly frustrating.

And she hated that she cared.

With a frustrated sigh, she retrieved a small journal from her satchel, flipping it open to a blank page.

She needed to get her thoughts down—to make sense of the puzzle that was Lucas Wycliffe.

Her pencil hovered over the page, the tip pressing lightly against the parchment.

She wrote two words.

Why him?

She stared at the question, the weight of it sinking into her chest.

It wasn't supposed to be like this. This was meant to be just another assignment—a stepping stone back into the career she'd nearly lost.

And yet, every time Lucas looked at her like he saw something she didn't want to confront, it left her breathless. Every wall he built seemed to reveal not weakness—but pain. A kind of grief she recognized far too well.

She stared at the phrase for a long moment.

The answer was far more complicated than she was willing to admit.

And that?

That terrified her.

Chapter Nine

The morning had dawned clear and crisp, the sky a boundless canvas of pale blue stretching over Hawthorne Manor's sprawling estate. There had been no indication, no warning signs that by afternoon, Emma Ainsworth would find herself trapped inside the stables with Lucas Wycliffe—soaked to the bone, confined in close quarters, and wrestling with a tension that stole the very breath from the air.

She had been helping to muck out the stalls, a task she had begrudgingly grown accustomed to, when the first low rumble of thunder rolled through the valley.

Pausing, she turned toward the open barn doors.

The once-bright horizon had darkened to an ominous shade of grey; the gathering storm clouds heavy with the promise of a downpour.

Footsteps crunched over the gravel outside, and moments later, Lucas strode in from the pastures, his broad frame silhouetted against the storm-lit sky. His hat was pulled low over his brow, shielding his eyes, but Emma could still sense the quiet calculation in his expression.

"The storm is advancing faster than expected," he said, his voice calm but firm. "We must bring the horses in at once."

Emma wiped her hands against her skirts and nodded. "What would you have me do?"

Lucas's gaze lingered on her for a moment before he gave a sharp nod toward the far paddock.

"Help me gather the last of them before the rains strike."

She did not argue.

Together, they moved with purposeful urgency, guiding the skittish horses toward the safety of the barn.

The winds picked up swiftly, a violent gust tearing through the valley, yanking strands of Emma's loosely pinned hair from their careful arrangement. The sky had blackened now, the trees along the fence line bending under the force of the approaching storm.

One particularly stubborn mare fought against Emma's lead, its hooves stamping restlessly against the dampening ground.

"Easy, girl," she murmured, tightening her grip on the reins, but the mare reared slightly, resisting.

Lucas was beside her in an instant.

Without hesitation, he placed a steadying hand over hers, his grip firm, reassuring.

"Lower your voice," he instructed. "Slow your movements."

Emma swallowed, nodding, adjusting her stance as Lucas did the same.

Together, they coaxed the mare forward, step by step, until, at last, she crossed the threshold of the stable doors.

And then—

The heavens split open.

The rain came down in torrents, crashing against the roof of the stable, drumming against the wooden beams in a deafening rhythm.

The storm rolled in with a fury that seemed to echo something unspoken between them—wild, untamed, and impossible to ignore.

Each drop that struck the wood felt like a heartbeat. A reminder that some forces couldn't be controlled—no matter how hard she tried to hold her distance from Lucas Wycliffe.

Emma turned—only to realize, in that moment, that she and Lucas were now alone.

Trapped in the storm.

And, judging by the sheer force of the rain?

They were not going anywhere anytime soon.

✿

"Move!"

Lucas's strong hand wrapped around her wrist, pulling her forward as the rain lashed against them in fierce, relentless waves.

The sky had split open, releasing a deluge so heavy it nearly stole the breath from her lungs.

By the time they reached the smaller supply barn just across the yard, Emma was half-blind from the downpour. Lucas wrenched open the doors, shoving her inside before following swiftly and slamming them shut behind them.

The thunder rumbled like a cannon's roar, and for a long moment, neither of them spoke—nor moved.

Water dripped from their clothes, pooling on the dusty wooden floor.

Emma shivered, swiping a trembling hand over her face to clear the wet strands clinging to her skin.

"Well." She exhaled, trying for lightness. "That was dramatic."

Lucas grunted, saying nothing as he shrugged out of his drenched coat and peeled off his soaked linen shirt, tossing it carelessly onto a nearby wooden crate.

Emma's breath hitched.

She tore her gaze away immediately, pretending the sight of him—bare forearms, soaked undershirt clinging to the firm cut of his frame, body heat radiating into the small space—wasn't doing strange, unwelcome things to her pulse.

Focus, Emma.

Folding her arms tightly across her chest, she tried to suppress the deep chill seeping into her bones. "So… what now?"

Lucas ran a hand through his wet hair, shaking out the droplets like a restless beast. "We wait."

Outside, the wind howled, rattling the wooden beams of the barn as the rain pounded mercilessly overhead.

The storm had enclosed them in their own little world.

Emma rubbed her arms, trying in vain to summon warmth.

Lucas noticed.

He shouldn't have cared. But when he saw her shiver—the vulnerability she tried so hard to conceal—something shifted inside him.

It wasn't pity. It was something worse. Something far more dangerous. A pull.

And Lucas knew better than to let anyone get close. Every person he had allowed near him had left eventually, taking pieces of him that never grew back.

With a sigh, he reached for a dry horse blanket from the nearby shelf and tossed it to her.

"Here. You're turning blue."

Emma caught it, mumbling a quick "Thank you."

She wrapped it around herself, inhaling the familiar scent of hay, leather, and… him.

Her stomach flipped in a way she did not appreciate.

The air between them grew heavier.

Neither of them spoke, the silence filled only by the steady drum of rain and the uneven rhythm of their breaths.

Emma risked a glance at him.

Lucas was watching her—his gaze lingering a second too long.

Her throat tightened.

"Are you always this charming in life-threatening situations?"

Lucas's lips curled into a slow, lazy smirk, the kind that sent an irritating flutter through her chest. "This ain't life-threatening, Ainsworth."

Emma huffed a small, breathy laugh, pulling the blanket tighter around her. "It feels a little dramatic, don't you think?"

Lucas didn't answer.

Instead, he took a single, slow step forward.

And just like that—the space between them felt nonexistent.

Emma's breath caught.

His hand lifted—hesitant, careful.

He was giving her time to pull away.

But she didn't.

She couldn't.

His fingertips brushed against her damp cheek, featherlight, fleeting.

The brush of his hand was both a question and a warning.

She should have pulled away. Instead, she leaned into it—just slightly, just enough to feel the warmth radiating from him despite the chill of the storm.

His thumb traced the faintest line along her cheekbone, and she could feel the hesitation in him, the battle between wanting and knowing better.

Every breath felt like a fragile thread stretched taut between them.

Emma swore the storm outside was nothing compared to whatever this was—whatever was crackling between them, electric and unspoken.

Her pulse thundered in her ears.

Lucas's gaze flickered to her lips.

And for the first time—perhaps ever—he looked as if he might finally close the distance.

Then—

A loud ring shattered the moment.

Lucas jerked back as if the contact had burned him, his jaw tightening instantly.

The withdrawal was swift—like slamming a door shut before it could swing open any farther.

He had almost lost control.

It wasn't supposed to happen—this wasn't what they

were supposed to be. She was meant to leave. And every second she stayed… every second he let his guard slip…

He couldn't afford it. Not again.

Emma blinked and snapped back into reality as the heavy silence collapsed around them.

Lucas dug into his pocket, pulling out his watch and flipping it open.

"Yes?" His voice was gruff, controlled—as if the last thirty seconds had never happened.

Emma took a slow step back, wrapping the blanket tighter around her like armor, her heart still hammering against her ribs.

She hadn't realized how close she had let herself get—until he pulled away.

It shouldn't hurt. Not this much. But it did.

The space between them now felt wider than the whole damn barn. And the worst part? She hadn't wanted him to let go.

Lucas's frown deepened.

"Damn it. Very well, I shall come at once."

He snapped the watch shut and turned to her, his expression unreadable once more.

"Something has happened in the village. We must leave."

Just like that, the storm was forgotten.

But the tension?

That remained.

Humming between them like an unanswered question.

Chapter Ten

The Harvest Fayre at Dunster was the sort of quaint, bustling affair that Emma had spent years convincing herself she had neither the time nor the inclination for.

And yet—here she was.

The air was thick with the scent of spiced cider and roasted chestnuts, mingling with the faint strains of violin music drifting from the village square. Soft golden lanterns hung from the twisted boughs of ancient oaks, their flickering light casting a warm, enchanted glow over the gathering.

A carousel spun lazily at the center of the square, children laughing gaily as they clung to their painted horses. Stalls lined the cobblestone streets, their vendors offering sugared almonds, fresh pastries, and handcrafted trinkets.

And somehow—against all odds—Lucas Wycliffe was here.

Emma had spent years convincing herself she didn't belong in this kind of life anymore. The cheerful noise, the warm familiarity of neighbors, the feeling of being remembered—it was unsettling. She had told herself that London's chaos was where she belonged, far from the quiet embrace of a village that knew her name. And yet, under the soft glow of lanterns, the threads of her past tugged at her heart with gentle persistence—unraveling all her carefully constructed distance.

And then, as if summoned by some unseen force tethering her to this place—Lucas Wycliffe was here.

It had taken more than a little persuasion.

A great deal of persistence.

And—if she were honest with herself—a carefully placed challenge to his pride.

"One evening," she had told him earlier, arms crossed, chin tilted up in defiance. "You shall endure but one evening without pretending to be a recluse."

Lucas had grumbled something about crowded streets and meaningless revelry, but in the end—he had relented.

And now?

Now, he stood beside her near the harvest stalls, hands buried deep in the pockets of his waistcoat, expression as unreadable as ever.

His usual scowl had softened, though—his gaze sweeping over the festivities with something almost resembling amusement.

Emma elbowed him playfully.

"You appear almost entertained, Mr. Wycliffe."

Lucas arched a single brow, casting her a sideways glance.

"I appear as though I would rather be anywhere else."

Emma smirked. "Close enough."

Despite his numerous grumblings and half-hearted protests, Lucas did not leave.

Lucas told himself it was the obligation of the evening that kept him by her side—nothing more. Yet every shared glance, every unexpected laugh, chipped away at the barriers he had built. He wasn't supposed to enjoy her company. And yet, with each passing moment, her presence felt less like an intrusion and more like… an anchor.

He trailed beside her as she wandered through the fayre, watching with quiet amusement as she tried—and failed—to master quoits.

She sampled mulled wine, wincing at its sweetness, and, to his visible displeasure, managed to convince him onto a hay cart, where they endured the chatter of the village's most insistent gossips as the cart rattled its way through the torch-lit streets.

And for all his grousing, for all his claims that he despised such social indulgences…

Lucas remained at her side.

And that, more than anything, unsettled her.

Emma was not accustomed to this.

Not to his presence at her shoulder without that familiar distance.

Not to the way he seemed… comfortable, even here, amidst the lanterns and the laughter.

Not to the way it made her feel—

Warm.

As if, perhaps, she belonged here, in this moment, more than she had ever realized.

They wandered toward the main stage, where couples moved in lazy circles across a wooden dance floor, the glow of hanging lanterns casting golden halos over their faces.

Emma stopped abruptly.

"Oh no."

Lucas frowned. "What now?"

She turned to him with a look of exaggerated distress.

"I have made a grave error."

Lucas's frown deepened. "What?"

She motioned toward the dance floor. "I struck a bargain with Mrs. Linton, the vicar's wife."

Lucas's expression darkened instantly. "What kind of bargain?"

Emma clasped her hands behind her back, rocking slightly on her heels.

"If I succeeded in getting you here, you were to dance."

Lucas's face flatlined.

"You did what?"

Emma grinned, extending her hand. "Come now, Mr. Wycliffe. A bargain is a bargain."

Lucas eyed her outstretched hand as though it concealed a dagger.

"I do not dance."

Emma arched a brow. "You manage an entire estate, work with horses daily, and you expect me to believe you cannot move in time to a melody?"

His lips pressed into a firm, disapproving line. "That is different."

"How so?"

He exhaled sharply, clearly fighting the urge to turn on his heel and walk away.

Emma took a step closer, her voice lowering.

"One dance. No one is watching."

Lucas's gaze flickered over the crowded square.

The look he gave her clearly conveyed his belief that she was utterly mad if she thought no one was watching.

And yet—

He took her hand.

His fingers were warm, firm, steady against her own.

His touch sent a ripple through her—a warmth that seeped beneath her skin, unsettling in its intensity. Emma had danced with men before, but never had something as simple as the brush of fingertips felt so… personal. As if, in that moment, Lucas Wycliffe wasn't just taking her hand. He was holding something far more fragile—her trust.

Emma's breath caught.

She had won the battle.

But suddenly—she wasn't so sure she was ready for the war.

The moment Lucas guided her onto the dance floor, Emma felt it.

The shift.

The undeniable pull.

The way her pulse faltered when his hands came to rest at her waist—firm, steady, as if they had always belonged there.

They moved slowly, swaying in time with the soft melody of the violin, the world narrowing to just the two of them and the golden glow of lanterns swaying in the evening breeze.

Emma swallowed hard, her breath hitching when Lucas's thumb brushed lightly against the small of her back.

The touch was nothing.

And yet—it was everything.

"See?" she whispered, attempting to infuse her tone with lightness, despite the rapid staccato of her heart.

"Not so dreadful after all."

Lucas did not respond.

He simply watched her.

Every instinct told him to let go, to keep the walls firmly in place. But as her hand rested lightly in his, and her breath brushed warm across his skin, something inside him began to unravel. She was a complication—a risk he couldn't afford. Yet standing here, the soft notes of the violin weaving around them, Lucas couldn't help but wonder what it might feel like to stop running.

His gaze—intense, searching—held something deep and unreadable, something that made heat curl low in her stomach.

And then—

He leaned in.

Slow.

Deliberate.

A question more than a demand.

And Emma?

She had the answer before he had even finished asking.

Her lashes fluttered shut, her breath stilling as she closed the distance, her lips grazing his in the softest, lightest of touches—

And then he kissed her back.

Deep.

Unhurried.

Certain.

It wasn't the rush of a sudden impulse—it was the slow recognition of something inevitable. His hand slid from her waist to the curve of her neck, fingers curling gently against her skin, grounding her in the reality of the moment. She had never been kissed like this. Not with such certainty, not with such quiet promise—like every broken piece of her could somehow be made whole again.

It was not fireworks, nor reckless abandon.

It was warmth.

A slow-burning fire in the middle of a cold night.

Emma had kissed before.

But never like this.

Never like it meant something.

Her fingers curled into the fabric of Lucas's coat, holding on—as if she were uncertain she could stand on her own should she let go.

And Lucas?

Lucas kissed her like a man who had spent far too long locking himself away—

And was finally, finally, letting someone in.

✾

Then—just as suddenly as it had begun—

Emma's pocket vibrated.

A sharp, unnatural jolt against the hush of the moment.

The spell snapped.

Emma jerked back, breath uneven, heart pounding, as she fumbled for the small, metal-clasped letter case she had tucked within her reticule.

Her editor's note.

The wax seal had already been broken, the parchment inside folded hastily, the ink scrawled in a hurried hand.

The paper trembled in her hands, though whether from cold or dread, she couldn't tell. The words blurred at first, as if her mind refused to process the cruel timing of the universe. The warmth of Lucas's kiss still lingered on her lips—how could something so simple, so pure, collide with the brutal reality she had tried so hard to ignore?

Her stomach turned to lead.

Lucas's brows knitted together. "What is it?"

Emma's fingers trembled over the parchment, her pulse a deafening roar in her ears.

The message was short. Brutal.

Miss Ainsworth, we have uncovered something on Lucas Wycliffe. Make haste to respond.

The laughter of the fayre faded into a distant hum, her entire world shrinking to that single line.

To the man standing in front of her.

To the warmth still lingering where his hands had been.

No.

Not now.

Not after this.

Lucas's gaze darkened, searching hers. "Emma?"

His voice was gentle—softer than she had ever heard it before. A tether pulling her back from the storm brewing within her. But she couldn't meet his eyes. Not now. Because if she did… she feared he might see the truth written across her face. The betrayal she had never intended. His voice was steady.

She looked up at him, torn between the weight of what had just transpired and the storm she could feel looming on the horizon.

She had wanted this night to be perfect.

But now?

Now, everything was about to fall apart.

Emma clutched the letter tighter, as if she could somehow crush the weight of its meaning. The warmth of Lucas's hand on her waist was gone now, replaced by the cold, suffocating knowledge that whatever this had been—it couldn't last.

And as the laughter of the fayre roared back to life around her, she realized one cruel, undeniable truth:

She hadn't just found a story in Lucas Wycliffe.

She had found something she wasn't ready to lose.

Chapter Eleven

The sealed letter in Emma's grasp might as well have been weighted with iron.

Her editor's message was short—too short, too sharp.

Miss Ainsworth, we have uncovered something about Lucas Wycliffe. Make haste to respond.

The words pressed against her ribs, heavy, suffocating.

She had wanted just one evening.

One evening where she need not think of deadlines, of obligations, of the past Lucas so determinedly kept locked away.

But reality had no patience for such indulgences.

It had come barreling into her world, tearing through the fragile moment she had allowed herself to believe in.

Even now, she could still feel him.

The warmth of his hands against her waist.

The way his lips had brushed against hers—slow, deliberate, reverent.

The way he had held her, as though she were something precious, something he was not yet ready to relinquish.

And now—

In the space of a single message, all of it threatened to crumble.

§

Emma did not immediately summon a messenger to return word to her editor.

She could not.

Instead, she stood frozen, the edges of the parchment crumpling slightly in her grip, her pulse a thundering echo in her ears.

Every fiber of her being screamed at her to protect him. How could she betray the man who had given her glimpses of vulnerability so few had ever seen? But then, the voice of her ambition—sharp, insistent—cut through her hesitation. This was her chance to prove herself, to salvage the career that had been teetering on the edge of collapse for far too long. Was her future worth the price of his past?

The fayre carried on around her, a swirl of laughter, golden lanterns, and soft violin strains.

She felt Lucas's gaze on her—steady, sharp, questioning.

"Emma?" His voice was low, measured. "What is the matter?"

She forced a smile—but it was thin, fragile. A poor imitation of something real.

"Nothing. Merely work."

Lucas did not look convinced.

But—for now—he did not press.

Instead, he inclined his head. "You would prefer to leave?"

Emma hesitated.

Every part of her screamed to say yes.

To let this evening be what it was meant to be.

But the letter in her palm was a crack in the illusion—a reminder that nothing was ever simple.

Still—for this moment, at least—she could pretend.

She nodded.

"Yes. Let us go."

Lucas did not hesitate.

With a light touch at her back, he guided her away from the fayre's glow, leading her back toward the darkened fields and quiet expanse of the manor's estate.

And as they walked beneath the vast stretch of starlit sky, Emma could not shake the creeping certainty that everything between them was about to change.

Emma stood outside the guesthouse, the crisp night air whispering against her skin, yet she felt nothing of it.

A single tallow candle flickered dimly from within, casting its wavering glow across the stone path.

Her fingers gripped the brass receiver, the metal cold against her palm as she held it to her ear.

She should have ignored the summons.

Should have left the note unread.

Should have let herself linger in the warmth of whatever had begun to take root between her and Lucas.

But she had not.

And now—

Now, she was listening to her editor drop a bomb upon the fragile world she had allowed herself to step into.

"His brother, Miss Ainsworth. The man has a brother."

Emma's breath stilled.

"I… I know."

A lie.

She did not know.

Lucas had never once mentioned a brother.

Jacob Wycliffe.

The name alone sent a ripple of unease through her chest.

Her editor's voice came sharp, urgent.

"The accident— it was not merely his."

Emma's grip tightened around the receiver.

Her pulse hammered.

"Jacob was involved, too. And what we have uncovered… it was not merely a career-ending injury, Emma. There is more."

Emma pressed a shaking hand to her forehead, her mind racing.

She did not want to hear this.

She did not want to know.

Not like this.

Not when she could still taste the memory of Lucas's lips upon hers, still feel the way his hands had held her as though she was something precious.

"What happened?"

The words slipped out before she could stop them.

A pause.

A silence that stretched too long, too weighted.

And then—

The truth unraveled.

❦

Five years ago.

Lucas and Jacob Wycliffe had been on the cusp of greatness—brothers bound not just by blood but by ambition, rivalry, and an unyielding pursuit of victory.

They had been set to compete in the most prestigious equestrian championship in the country—a chance to etch their names into history.

But then—

The accident.

A late-night training session.

One wrong move.

One miscalculated jump.

Jacob had been thrown. Hard.

The impact had been merciless—his leg crushed beneath the weight of his own mount, the bones shattering like brittle glass. A single, brutal instant had stolen everything.

His future.

His legacy.

His very ability to ride again.

Lucas had tried to save him.

Had thrown himself toward his brother in desperation—only to fall too.

Though Lucas had risen—bruised, battered, but whole—Jacob had not.

Jacob had lost more than a competition.

He had lost everything.

And Lucas?

He had never forgiven himself.

Emma exhaled, the weight of it pressing heavily upon her chest.

This was why he had walked away.

Not just from the sport.

Not just from his ambitions.

But from everything.

Emma barely registered her editor's voice as it droned on, the words filtering through the static of her thoughts.

"You need to write this story, Miss Ainsworth. The people will want to know the truth of Lucas Wycliffe."

Lucas Wycliffe.

Not the man who had just held her upon the dance floor.

Not the man who had kissed her as though she were the only thing tethering him to this world.

No—

To them, he was just another headline.

Another scandal to be unearthed.

Another name to be exposed.

Emma shut her eyes.

"I need time," she murmured.

A pause.

Then, a long, resigned sigh.

"Do not take too long."

A beat.

"If we do not move on this, someone else will."

The line went dead.

And Emma was left standing alone in the night, caught between duty… and something far more dangerous.

❦

Emma had not realized how long she had stood frozen in place, staring into the night, until she heard the crunch of boots upon gravel.

A slow, steady cadence—measured, deliberate.

She turned.

Lucas.

The moment their eyes met, she knew—he saw it.

The hesitation.

The doubt.

And just like that—the walls went up.

His expression hardened.

His posture shifted—no longer open, no longer searching—but guarded. Cold.

"You are going to tell me what troubles you, are you not?" His voice was even. Controlled.

Emma hesitated, fingers tightening around the folded letter still clutched in her grasp.

She wanted to tell him.

But if she did—if she uttered a single word of what she had learned—

It would ruin everything.

So she did the only thing she could.

She lied.

"It is nothing."

Lucas did not move.

Did not blink.

For a moment, the slightest flicker of hurt crossed his face—barely there, gone in a heartbeat—but she saw it. And that hurt, that shadow of disappointment, cut deeper than any accusation. His jaw tightened, and something inside him shuttered, closing off the fragile thread of connection they had only just begun to build.

He regarded her intently, his silence a tangible force between them—unspoken, yet demanding a response.

And then—he did what he always did.

He pulled away.

✤

The following day, everything was different.

Lucas kept his distance.

Emma felt it in the way he did not meet her eyes.

In the way, his words came clipped, sharp, and short.

In the rigid set of his shoulders as he worked with the horses—his focus poured into anything, into everything, except her.

He knew.

Perhaps not the details.

But he knew she was hiding something.

And Lucas Wycliffe did not abide secrets.

Emma sat upon the fence post near the paddock, watching him wordlessly, helplessly, as he moved through his tasks with grim efficiency.

The ache in her chest wasn't just for him—it was for herself, too. A sharp memory clawed at her—the day she had first learned what betrayal felt like. London's sharp coldness, her editor's cold words after her last failed assignment: "You had potential, Ainsworth. A pity ambition was never enough." Now, she was standing on the edge of a familiar cliff, about to lose something she hadn't even realized she wanted to keep.

And in that moment—she realized something with startling, undeniable clarity.

She had two choices.

She could tell him the truth.

Or she could watch him walk away—for good.

And this time—

She might not be able to bring him back.

Chapter Twelve

Emma knew she could not hold this secret much longer.

The knowledge of Lucas's past, the accident, the brother he had never once spoken of—

It sat in her chest like a stone, weighing her down with each step she took, each moment she spent in his presence.

She saw it in the way he watched her now, how the warmth of their unspoken connection had faltered, replaced by something colder, warier.

Lucas Wycliffe had once begun to let her in.

But now, his guard was up again—stronger than before.

He knew something was wrong.

And if she did not tell him the truth now—she might

never have another chance.

The afternoon sun dipped low, casting long golden shadows over Hawthorne Manor's sprawling grounds.

Every moment she hesitated felt like a betrayal. The words weighed heavily on her tongue, thick with guilt and fear. How could she undo the damage of knowing something she was never meant to discover? She could still feel the ghost of his hands on her waist, the warmth of his breath against her skin—but now, it all felt like borrowed time, moments stolen under false pretenses.

Emma found Lucas by the paddock, adjusting the reins on one of the younger horses.

He looked like he belonged there.

The breeze lifted the dark strands of his hair, the late-day light accentuating the sharp angles of his face, the quiet strength in his hands.

For a moment, she allowed herself to simply look at him.

Not as a journalist. Not as a story.

But as a man.

A man who had become so much more than she ever intended.

And that made what she had to do all the more difficult.

Emma swallowed, forcing her feet to move forward.

"Lucas."

His shoulders tensed slightly before he turned, his gaze steady, expectant.

"Yes?"

She hesitated.

One last chance to turn away, to bury this truth and let it remain in the dark.

But she couldn't.

Not anymore.

Emma drew in a breath, willing her voice to remain steady.

"I know about Jacob."

Lucas's entire body went still.

The relaxed stance, the quiet ease with which he had leaned against the fence—all of it vanished in an instant.

His gaze turned cold. Hard.

"What did you just say?"

Emma licked her lips, choosing her words with care.

"Your brother, Jacob. The accident. I—I found out."

Silence.

A long, stifling silence stretched between them like an open chasm.

Lucas's hands slowly curled into fists, his knuckles going white.

"Who told you?"

His voice was too quiet. Too controlled.

But Emma felt the tension behind it.

The weight of something dangerous and unspoken.

She could lie.

Tell him she had come across an old article.

That she had overheard a passing remark in the village.

But Lucas Wycliffe despised lies.

So she told the truth.

"My editor," she admitted, voice barely above a whisper. "They did some digging. I—I did not ask them to, but they uncovered it. And they told me."

Lucas let out a slow, measured breath.

Then—he laughed.

A sharp, bitter sound.

The sound was more than bitter—it was hollow. A defense, sharp and jagged, meant to keep her at bay. His eyes darkened, not with anger, but with something colder: disappointment. "Of course. Of course, you found out. Everyone always does—eventually." The words fell from his lips like a verdict, final and unforgiving.

Emma stepped forward.

"Lucas—"

"How long?"

His gaze locked onto hers, piercing, unrelenting.

"How long have you known?"

Emma's throat tightened.

"Since the night of the fayre."

Since the night we kissed.

Something in his expression flickered.

Hurt.

Disappointment.

Betrayal.

❦

"So that is why you have been acting differently."

Lucas's voice had taken on an edge, a roughness she had never heard before.

Emma shook her head. "It is not like that."

"Is it not?"

He took a step closer, his presence looming, suffocating.

"You learned about Jacob, and suddenly, you start looking at me differently. You hesitate. And now, what? You come to me, feigning concern, pretending you give a damn about the truth?"

"I do care."

Emma's voice cracked.

"That is why I am telling you."

Lucas's jaw tensed, his muscles coiling tight.

He turned away, running a rough hand through his hair, pacing once before stopping abruptly.

"You should go."

The words hit her like a slap.

Emma's chest tightened.

"Lucas—"

"Go."

His voice was flat. Final.

A command.

Not a plea.

Not a request.

Emma felt anger flare beneath the hurt.

But beneath the anger was something worse—guilt. She had never meant for it to unravel this way. She wasn't just fighting for the truth anymore; she was fighting to prove she wasn't like the others who had taken pieces of him and left him hollow. She wanted to prove that she was different. That she cared. But how could she convince him of that when she wasn't even sure she believed it herself?

"I am trying to talk to you! Why must you always do this? Why must you shut down the moment something becomes too real?"

Lucas turned back to her, his eyes flashing with something raw. Something dangerous.

"Perhaps because I do not wish for my life to be dissected like some front-page scandal."

The words cut deep.

Emma took a step back.

"Is that what you believe this to be?" she whispered.

Lucas did not blink.

Did not hesitate.

"Is it not?"

Emma inhaled sharply. "You do not mean that."

Lucas let out another bitter laugh.

"Do I not?"

He stepped closer, and for the first time since she had met him, Emma felt the full weight of his walls closing in.

"Tell me something, Miss Ainsworth."

His voice was low, steady, deadly soft.

"Had I not kissed you, would you still be here? Would you still be playing this game, pretending you cared? Or would you have already written your article and left?"

Emma felt as though he had struck her.

She wanted to scream at him, to tell him he was wrong.

To tell him that what had transpired between them had been real.

But the doubt had already seeped in.

Lucas Wycliffe did not believe her.

And perhaps—

Perhaps he never would.

❧

Lucas turned away once more, his breath measured, controlled—too controlled.

Emma knew.

He was done.

She could feel it, like a chill in the marrow of her bones.

Her throat tightened. "I was not going to write about it."

Lucas stilled.

For the briefest moment—a mere heartbeat, a whisper of hesitation—she thought he might turn.

But he did not.

His back remained rigid, his shoulders locked in unrelenting tension.

Emma swallowed past the lump in her throat.

"I was not going to publish it, Lucas. I only—" her voice wavered, but she forced herself to continue, "I only wished to understand."

Silence.

The worst kind of silence.

Then, finally, Lucas spoke.

"You ought to have left it alone."

And just like that—he walked away.

His footsteps faded into the stillness of the evening, swallowed by the vast expanse of land, by the unforgiving quiet that stretched between them.

Lucas didn't look back, but she saw it—the slight falter in his step, the moment of hesitation that betrayed how much this hurt him too. He wasn't walking away because he didn't care—he was walking away because he cared too much and didn't know how to survive it. And that realization made her heart ache in a way that no rejection ever had before.

Emma watched him go, her chest tightening with a pain so sharp, so relentless, it felt as though she had just lost something she never truly had.

But she couldn't let this be the end. Not yet. The sting of rejection burned through her, yes—but beneath it was something stronger. A stubborn, reckless need to make things right. Lucas had built walls so high even the truth couldn't climb over them, but she had seen what lay beneath—vulnerability, loyalty, and pain that ran deeper than any headline could capture. She couldn't walk away now. Not when she knew the man he truly was beneath all that silence and solitude.

⚜

That night, Emma sat alone in her chambers, staring at the blank page of parchment before her.

Her editor had called again.

She had not answered.

She could still hear Lucas's words, the finality in them.

Tell me something, Miss Ainsworth. Had I not kissed you, would you still be here?

She hated that he had asked it.

Hated it even more that she did not know the answer.

Because if she was honest with herself—if she stripped away all pretenses, all justifications—

She had never expected to stay.

Not truly.

She had come to Dunster for a story.

And somewhere along the way—against all reason, against all self-preservation—

She had begun to hope for something more.

And now?

Now, she had lost everything.

And the worst part?

She had no one to blame but herself.

Chapter Thirteen

Heartbreak, Emma had always believed, was a thing of violence.

A thing of raised voices and shattered glass, of lovers parting beneath the weight of harsh words and bitter farewells.

She had imagined it to be loud.

Messy. Uncontrollable.

But this?

This was silence.

It was waking to the same village, yet feeling as though it no longer belonged to her.

It was passing by Hawthorne Manor, knowing she would not step foot upon its land again.

Knowing she would not see Lucas standing by the paddock, the crisp wind catching in his dark hair.

Knowing she would not hear his gruff orders or his maddeningly rare moments of teasing amusement.

It was the aching weight in her chest, the stinging behind her eyes, the unbearable truth that she had lost him.

Or perhaps—

She had never had him at all.

And the worst part?

Lucas did not even seem to care.

❦

She had gone to the manor that morning.

She had not known precisely what she had hoped for—

A conversation.

A chance at closure.

She had spent half the night staring at the ceiling, replaying their quarrel, reliving every word he had hurled at her.

Every moment of that cold, brutal silence when he had looked upon her and decided—decided that she was no better than every other journalist who had come sniffing about his past.

Perhaps she should have fought harder.

Perhaps she should have seized his hand, forced him to listen, made him understand—

That it was not about an article.

That it was not about the damned story.

That it was about him.

About her.

About the impossible thing that had been growing between them from the very first moment their eyes had met.

But when she arrived—

She had never even been given the chance.

Lucas had not come to the door.

Instead, one of the estate workers—Nathaniel—had met her upon the steps.

His hat was in hand, his expression awkward, pitying.

"My apologies, Miss Ainsworth." His voice was gentle, hesitant. "Mr. Wycliffe instructed that the interviews shall not continue."

That was all.

No explanations.

No arguments.

No chance to make things right.

Only a message—delivered through another man's lips.

Lucas had cut her out completely.

Emma felt the tightness in her throat.

She managed a numb nod, an empty smile.

"I understand."

Her voice sounded foreign to her own ears.

And then she turned—

And walked away.

She forced herself not to look back.

Forced herself to pretend it did not hurt.

But it did.

God, it did.

Drowning in Regret

Emma sat within the dim-lit corner of Dunster's modest tea house, staring absently at the delicate porcelain cup before her.

The tea had long since cooled, its surface untouched, the fragrant steam now nothing more than a faint memory.

Beside it, upon the table, lay her neglected calling card case.

Her editor had sent word twice.

She had not answered.

She ought to have felt triumphant.

She had obtained what she had come for.

She had gathered more than enough material to craft a compelling, career-defining piece—

The tale of Lucas Wycliffe, the fallen prodigy, the former equestrian champion who had disappeared from the world, only to resurface upon an unassuming estate cloaked in secrecy, buried beneath his past.

She could leave this very evening.

Return to London, to her life, to the world she had so

carefully built for herself.

Publish the article.

And never look back.

That had been the plan all along.

Had it not?

So why, then, did the mere thought of departing leave her feeling as though she were drowning in regret?

Why did it feel as though she were making the gravest mistake of her life?

❦

The realization struck with the force of a slap.

She was in love with him.

Not merely captivated.

Not merely intrigued by the brooding, unreadable nature of the man.

It was not attraction alone, nor was it simply the thrill of proximity or the pull of a challenge.

It was real.

And it was devastating.

Because she had already lost him.

Emma let out a shaky breath, her fingers lifting to press against her temple.

She had spent her entire life believing that love was a thing for others.

A thing for poets and dreamers, for reckless hearts and foolish minds.

She had seen her parents' union fracture, had watched her mother waste away in sorrow for years after, had sworn to herself—sworn—that she would never be so careless, never place her future in the hands of another.

And yet—here she sat.

Alone.

In a village where she had no claim.

In a place, she had no reason to remain.

Aching for a man who had already decided—conclusively, irrevocably—that she was not worth the risk

The evening air was crisp as Emma walked aimlessly through Dunster's quiet streets, the glow of gas lamps flickering against the cobblestone paths.

She hadn't meant to stop at the bakery, but somehow, she found herself there—standing in the doorway, hands trembling at her sides.

Mrs.Pembroke, looked up from behind the counter, her knowing eyes softening at the sight of Emma.

"Oh, my dear." She wiped her hands on her apron, stepping around the counter. "You look as if someone's taken the last bit of light from your heart."

Emma let out a breathless laugh, blinking away the sting behind her eyes. "Something like that."

Mrs.Pembroke tilted her head. "Come in, then. You look like you could use a cup of tea—and a bit of truth."

They sat at the small wooden table near the bakery window, the scent of warm bread wrapping around Emma like a fragile comfort.

Mrs. Pembroke took a sip of her tea, watching her carefully. "You're leaving."

Emma stilled. "How did you—"

"Because I was young once, too." A small smile. "And because when a woman wears that look on her face—the one that says she's torn between her heart and her pride—she's usually already made up her mind."

Emma swallowed, staring into her own untouched cup. "He doesn't want me."

Mrs. Pembroke sighed. "Ah. So you're running."

Emma's head snapped up. "I am not running."

Mrs. Pembroke simply lifted a brow.

Emma clenched her jaw. "He—he made his choice."

"And did you ever give him a chance to make another?"

Emma opened her mouth, then closed it.

Mrs. Pembroke leaned forward, voice gentler now. "Listen to me, child. Love is a foolish thing, sometimes. It makes men push people away when all they really want to do is pull them close. It makes women leave before they've given someone the chance to stop them."

Emma exhaled shakily. "I don't want to beg him to love me."

Mrs. Pembroke's expression softened. "Begging ain't

the same as fighting for something worth having."

Silence.

Emma traced the rim of her cup, her throat tightening. "What if I stay, and he never lets me in?"

Mrs.Pembroke set her tea down, reaching across the table to take Emma's hand. "Then you'll know you fought for it. And sometimes, my dear, that's enough."

Emma stood in the middle of her small rented chambers, staring at the half-filled travel trunk upon the bed, her hands clenched into fists at her sides.

She had booked passage back to London that very morning.

The ticket sat heavy in her pocket, a promise of escape she wasn't ready to keep. Her mind whispered all the reasons why leaving was the logical choice—her career, her reputation, the chance to walk away with her pride intact.

But her heart, traitorous and stubborn, screamed louder. Every inch of this village held a piece of her now—the scent of fresh earth on the manor grounds, the soft cadence of Lucas's voice when he wasn't shielding himself behind silence, the warmth of his hands steady on her waist.

To leave would mean letting go of more than just a story. It would mean letting go of him.

It was the sensible course of action.

There was nothing left for her here.

Lucas had made it abundantly clear that whatever had passed between them—whatever fragile, unspoken thing had existed in the space between their words and glances—

It was over.

And yet—

Each time she reached for another article of clothing, prepared to fold it into the trunk's waiting emptiness, her fingers stilled, her body refusing to obey.

Her hand brushed against the edge of her desk, grazing the folded handkerchief Lucas had given her the day she first stumbled over that cursed fence. She picked it up, running her fingers over the worn fabric. The faintest trace of lavender—his scent—still lingered in the fibers. Her heart twisted painfully. The room felt too quiet without the memory of his voice, too still without the warmth of his gaze. The ache in her chest deepened as she forced herself to fold the handkerchief and place it in her trunk.

She did not wish to leave.

She did not wish to leave this village, this estate, this man.

But what was the alternative?

Stay—and pray that Lucas might forgive her?

Stay—and attempt to mend something that he had already deemed irreparable?

No.

She had to go.

She knew that.

She simply did not know how to make herself do it.

That evening, just as the sun dipped beyond the distant hills, Emma found herself standing outside the gates of Hawthorne Manor for what she knew must be the final time.

The house stood silent, the great oak trees lining the drive casting long, dappled shadows in the fading light.

Beyond the manor walls, the horses grazed idly in the paddock, utterly unaffected by the weight pressing down upon her chest.

A lantern glowed softly within the open stable doors, its golden light spilling across the gravel path.

Everything looked precisely as it had before.

Unchanged. Unbothered.

Except—

He was not there.

Lucas Wycliffe was not there.

And he was not going to stop her.

For the briefest, most foolish of moments, she had let herself hope.

Hope that he might appear upon the steps, stride toward her with that same steady, determined gait that she had come to recognize as his own.

That he might say she was mistaken.

That he might say he could not let her go.

But Lucas Wycliffe did not chase people.

He let them go.

And he had let her go.

Emma swallowed against the aching lump in her throat, turned upon her heel—

And walked away.

Emma paused at the end of the long, winding road. One last glance back, foolish and futile. The manor stood silent, unmoved by her heartache. The glow from the stables flickered faintly in the distance—a reminder of what could have been. She wiped the sting from her eyes before it could fall, squared her shoulders, and kept walking. If Lucas wouldn't fight for her, she would not beg him to.

❧

Lucas stood at the edge of the paddock, his hands clenched into fists at his sides, watching as Emma's carriage disappeared down the winding road.

The sun dipped low over the paddocks, casting long shadows across the worn fields. Lucas remained frozen, every instinct screaming at him to move—go after her, say something, anything. But the weight of fear held him still. The wind stirred through the grass, carrying the ghost of her laughter through the air, leaving a hollow ache in his chest. How could something so simple feel like the end of everything?

He should have stopped her.

He knew it.

Every muscle in his body was coiled tight, every instinct screaming at him to go after her, to tell her that it hadn't all been a lie, that whatever had grown between them had been real—so much more real than he had ever been prepared for.

But he could not.

Not when the doubt still lingered.

Not when the memory of that conversation, of that single shattering revelation, still cut into him like a blade.

She had come here for a story.

Not for him.

Hadn't she?

Lucas exhaled sharply, his gaze locked upon the empty road, the evening air pressing heavy against his chest.

He wanted to believe her.

Wanted to believe that she had felt what he had felt.

That the night at the fayre, the way she had looked at him before he kissed her, had meant something.

But he had spent too many years learning the hard way that wanting something did not make it real.

So he let her go.

And when she was gone—

When the carriage had vanished beyond the bend, swallowed by the creeping darkness—

When the last traces of daylight slipped beneath the

horizon, leaving nothing but the cold hush of evening—

Lucas Wycliffe felt the loss like an open wound.

A wound he had no idea how to heal.

The echoes of her absence settled into the bones of Hawthorne Manor, filling every inch of silence with what could have been. The stables, once a refuge, now felt hollow—every creak of wood, every rustle of hay, a reminder of her laughter, her determination, her stubborn refusal to let him retreat. And now she was gone. And it was his fault.

And yet, as the night swallowed the last traces of daylight, Lucas knew he deserved every ounce of emptiness left in her wake.

Chapter Fourteen

For the entirety of her career, Miss Emma Ainsworth had pursued the singular ambition that drove all journalists of her standing—the story that would set her apart.

The one that would establish her name among the finest, the one that would cement her reputation, proving to the world—and to herself—that she was as relentless as any of the men who dominated her profession.

And now— at long last—she had it.

The scandal.

The fall from grace.

The tragic tale of a lost heir, a fallen prodigy, a man burdened by secrets.

And yet—

She could not write it.

Not the way they wanted.

Emma sat before the large oak writing desk in her London chambers, her fingers poised over the blank parchment, the ink-dipped quill hovering just above its pristine surface.

Her previous notes lay discarded, the outline of her article—the one detailing Lucas's past, the tragedy that had shaped him, the brother he had lost—still unfinished, untouched.

It was not the story she would tell.

Because the truth was not found in his mistakes or his misfortunes.

It was not in the scandalous whispers that editors so desperately craved.

Lucas Wycliffe deserved better.

❦

It had been three days since she had departed Dunster.

Three days since she had left Hawthorne Manor behind, since she had forced herself to walk away.

Three days of pretending that it had all meant nothing.

London's streets were as she had always known them to be—bustling, urgent, gleaming with the glow of gas lamps, carriages rolling steadily across damp cobblestones.

And yet, for the first time in her life, she did not feel as though she belonged.

She passed grand shopfronts, towering buildings, and

the ever-present hum of society's finest moving through their evening affairs—but it was all hollow.

Because home had not been here.

Home had been—

The quiet hush of dawn breaking over open fields.

The scent of leather and hay.

The sound of horses stirring in the paddock, the warmth of a fire burning low in the evening hearth.

Home had been the way Lucas Wycliffe had looked at her in the firelight, his guarded eyes flickering with something unspoken, something real, just before he had cast it aside and pushed her away.

Emma exhaled sharply, shaking her head, forcing herself to pull the parchment closer.

She had to write.

But not the article they wanted.

The article he deserved.

✤

Emma inhaled deeply, dipped her quill into the inkwell, and pressed its tip to the fine parchment before her.

She did not write of scandal or disgrace.

She did not write of a fallen champion nor of the dark whispers that had followed Lucas Wycliffe since the accident that had stolen his future.

Instead, she wrote of a man who had lost everything— and yet, somehow, had built something beautiful from the wreckage.

She wrote of a man who had turned his pain into purpose—who had rescued horses, given a home to the lost and the wounded, and offered second chances to creatures that the world had cast aside.

She wrote of his kindness—the way he protected all that he held dear, even if it meant keeping his own heart locked away.

She wrote of his strength, his patience, his unyielding devotion to the estate, to the village, to the people who still turned to him, even as he remained on the fringes of their world, watching, never fully stepping into the light.

She wrote of the way he had made her feel.

As though she belonged.

As though, for the first time in her life, she was not merely chasing stories—but rather, finding herself within one.

And then—

Finally—

She wrote the words she had been too afraid to say aloud.

She had fallen in love with him.

✷

The fire in the hearth burned low, casting flickering shadows against the walls of Emma's modest London chambers. Outside, the rain pattered softly against the windowpane, muffling the distant hum of carriage wheels and hurried footsteps on the cobblestone streets.

She had been staring at the manuscript for hours, her fingers trembling over the words she had just finished writing. Words not of scandal, not of a broken past, but of him—of Lucas Wycliffe, of the man she had come to know in the quiet hours of dawn, in the warmth of an evening fire, in the spaces where words were left unspoken but felt all the same.

She should have felt relief. The article was finished. It was not the exposé she had been sent to write, but it was the truth—the only truth that mattered.

And yet, the moment the ink dried, the unease in her chest did not fade.

A sharp knock at the door shattered the silence.

Emma startled, her pulse kicking up as she pushed back from the desk. For a brief moment, she hesitated. It was late. Who would be calling at such an hour?

She crossed the room, unfastening the latch, and found herself staring down at a damp-haired boy, no older than twelve, shivering in the hallway.

"Telegram for Miss Ainsworth," he announced, breathless, holding out a folded slip of paper.

Her stomach twisted.

She accepted the telegram, pressing a coin into the boy's palm before closing the door. The firelight flickered as she unfolded the thin sheet, her breath hitching as her gaze ran over the inked words.

MISS EMMA AINSWORTH

ARTICLE REMAINS UNPUBLISHED. EXPECTED SUBSTANCE NOT SENTIMENT. IF SUITABLE COPY NOT RECEIVED CONSIDER ASSIGNMENT FORFEIT. RESPOND AT ONCE.

H. WHITMORE

Emma's fingers tightened around the telegram.

A cold dread settled in her stomach.

She had known this was coming. Of course she had. She had written a love letter to a man who did not wish to be known, rather than the hard-hitting exposé they had demanded.

And now, she would pay the price for it.

She sank into her chair, staring at the words that all but sealed her fate. This was her last chance. If she walked away from this story, she wasn't just walking away from a headline—she was walking away from everything she had fought for.

Years of hard work. Every late night. Every rejected article.

This was supposed to be the one that changed everything.

But at what cost?

Her gaze flickered to the manuscript—the article that spoke not of scandal, but of a man who had built something beautiful from the wreckage of his past.

Lucas.

His name alone sent a sharp ache through her chest.

She had made her choice.

And now—she had to face the consequences.

The next morning, a dense fog clung to the streets of London, muffling the sounds of carriage wheels rattling over cobblestones and the hurried steps of businessmen disappearing into the gray haze.

Emma stepped out of the hansom cab, her heart a steady, uneasy drum against her ribs as she ascended the stone steps of The London Observer. The grand building loomed before her, its façade stark against the pale morning sky.

She had been here countless times before. But never like this.

Inside, the air smelled of ink and damp wool, the ever-present hum of clacking typewriters filling the corridors. The hurried movements of men in waistcoats and sleeves rolled to the elbow gave the place an air of barely contained chaos, yet Emma felt separate from it all—as if she were walking toward an execution rather than an editorial meeting.

A clerk glanced up as she passed, his eyes widening slightly before he quickly looked away.

They had read it.

She swallowed hard, smoothing her skirts as she

reached the heavy oak door at the end of the corridor. She hesitated only briefly before lifting a gloved hand and knocking.

A voice—sharp, clipped—answered from within. "Enter."

Emma inhaled deeply, braced herself, and stepped inside.

Mr. H. Whitmore, the Observer's senior editor, sat behind his imposing mahogany desk, his fingers steepled beneath his chin. The morning's newspaper lay spread before him, Emma's article prominently displayed.

His expression was unreadable.

"You received my telegram," he said coolly, gesturing to the chair before his desk.

Emma sat, clasping her hands tightly in her lap. "I did."

Whitmore exhaled slowly, tapping a finger against the newspaper. "This is not the piece we discussed."

Emma met his gaze, steady despite the churning in her stomach. "No. It isn't."

Whitmore's lips pressed into a thin line. "You were given a story of scandal, Miss Ainsworth. A man who had everything, lost it, and disappeared into obscurity. The accident. The estranged brother. That was the story we paid for."

Emma's jaw tightened. "I wrote the story that was true."

Whitmore let out a humorless chuckle, shaking his head. "Miss Ainsworth, truth and what sells are rarely the same thing."

Emma leaned forward, her pulse thrumming. "Then perhaps you should ask yourself why people care for scandal at all. Because it is not tragedy they hunger for—it is redemption."

Whitmore's brow arched, the only sign of interest he had shown thus far.

Emma pressed on. "Lucas Wycliffe was not a man hiding in disgrace—he was a man who had built something out of nothing. He was a man who had taken his pain and turned it into something good. Is that not a story worth telling?"

Whitmore studied her for a long moment, his shrewd gaze flickering over her face as though searching for some sign of hesitation.

And then—he sighed.

"You are fortunate," he said at last, folding the paper neatly. "The public has taken an interest in your romantic interpretation of this man's life. It is being read."

Emma barely had time to process the words before he continued.

"But do not mistake that for approval." His voice turned cool again. "You had the makings of a front-page scandal, and instead, you sent us a sentimental reflection. That is not the sort of journalism that sustains a career. Do not expect another assignment from this office."

The words should have devastated her.

For years, The London Observer had been her goal, her measure of success. And now, she was watching it slip through her fingers.

But as she sat there, staring at the man who had once been the gatekeeper to her future, she realized something.

She did not want another assignment from this office.

She did not want to spend her life chasing scandals that would be discarded with the next day's news.

She had found something more—something real.

And for the first time, she was choosing her own path.

Emma stood, smoothing her skirts. "Then it appears this is my last day at The Observer."

Whitmore studied her, his mouth twitching as though amused by her defiance. "So it appears."

Emma turned toward the door, her heart pounding, her hands trembling.

But she did not falter.

She walked out of the office, out of the building, and into the cold London morning—free, uncertain, but unburdened for the first time in her life.

❧

Lucas Wycliffe stood upon the front steps of Hawthorne Manor, staring at the land that stretched out before him.

The sky was painted in muted tones of gray and gold, the fields swaying gently in the late afternoon breeze. The world had not changed.

And yet—

Everything felt different.

She was gone.

And he hated how much he felt it.

He told himself it was for the best—that Emma Ainsworth had never belonged in his world. That she had come for a story, and she had left with one.

He told himself he did not care what she had written.

That it did not matter.

That she did not matter.

But the truth?

The truth was far more unbearable.

Because deep down—where he had long buried the parts of himself he did not wish to face—he had wanted her to fight for him.

To tell him she wasn't leaving.

To tell him he was worth staying for.

And she hadn't.

She had walked away.

And he—

He had let her.

✹

It was not until several days had passed, the morning mist still curling along the vast hills of Hawthorne , when Nate—the head stableman—appeared at the manor's entrance, a crisp, folded newspaper in his gloved hand.

Lucas Wycliffe had been in the stables, tending to one of the newly arrived mares, when the man's shadow darkened the doorway.

"Sir." Nate's voice was carefully neutral, but there was something in his gaze that made Lucas pause.

"What is it?" Lucas asked, brushing dust from his hands as he turned.

Nate extended the paper toward him. "Thought you might want to see this."

Lucas took the newspaper hesitantly.

And then—his breath stalled.

There, printed in bold, elegant lettering, was a name he had been trying—and failing—to forget.

Emma Ainsworth.

His chest tightened. God, he was not ready for this.

For whatever words she had written.

For whatever truth she had chosen to tell the world.

And yet, with something between dread and reluctant curiosity, he slowly unfolded the paper.

He braced himself.

For the worst.

For a scandal.

For a betrayal.

For words that would tear apart what little peace he had managed to salvage in her absence.

But what he found—was none of those things.

❧

It was not about the accident.

It was not about his brother.

It was not about his past at all.

Instead—

It was about him.

The man he had become.

She wrote of the estate, of the horses he had saved, of the young stable hands who had found a purpose within his gates.

She wrote of his quiet strength, of the way he built something from nothing, of the way he protected what he loved, even when it cost him everything.

She painted a portrait not of a broken man—but of a man worth knowing.

Lucas swallowed hard, his pulse hammering beneath his ribs.

And then—

At the very end of the article, he saw them.

Her words.

Words that were not for the world—

They were for him.

❧

I did not merely uncover a story in Hawthorne . I found a man who does not yet comprehend the weight of his own worth.

A man who shields his heart from the world and yet gives more of himself than most men ever do.

I left that place with one undeniable truth—

Lucas Wycliffe is the kind of man one does not forget.

The kind of man one does not stop caring for.

The kind of man—

One could love.

❧

Lucas stopped breathing.

Could love.

His eyes swept over the words again as if reading them twice would make them less real, less impossible.

Could love.

His fingers clenched the paper.

His heart slammed against his ribs.

For the first time since she had left—since she had stood before him with regret in her eyes, since he had let her go—Lucas felt something new.

Something that was not anger.

Something that was not regret.

Something that was not just loss.

It was a spark.

A small, flickering ember of something he had long forgotten how to feel.

Hope.

He exhaled sharply, shaking his head as if to clear it.

But the truth had already settled deep inside him, refusing to be ignored.

This wasn't over.

Not yet.

Lucas Wycliffe had spent too long letting people walk away.

And if Emma Ainsworth thought she could love him—

Then by God—

He was going to make damn sure she knew he loved her right back.

Chapter Fifteen

Lucas Wycliffe had always believed that the past was best left untouched.

It was easier that way.

Easier to continue forward without looking back, to let old wounds calcify into something one could bear, something that no longer had the power to hurt. Easier to convince oneself that the weight of regret was merely another burden to be endured—one more brick in the foundation of solitude.

But now, as he sat upon the grand veranda of Hawthorne Manor, the morning sun casting long golden streaks over the rolling pastures, his hands gripped the edges of the newspaper before him as though it might vanish into the breeze.

The weight of regret settled on his chest, a heaviness

that made every breath feel like a struggle. His eyes drifted beyond the veranda toward the stables, where he had first seen Emma brushing Daisy, her stubborn determination radiating from every movement. A muscle ticked in his jaw. The memory was vivid—her laughter, her warmth, the way she challenged him without fear. And now, he realized, every moment she had spent trying to know him was a chance he had thrown away. His hand crumpled the newspaper as a surge of panic clawed at his chest. He couldn't let her slip away. Not again.

For the first time in years, the past was not what threatened to undo him.

He was.

The article lay open upon the wooden table, the inked words precise, deliberate—a mirror turned toward his own reflection. Miss Emma Ainsworth had penned her story with the same unyielding resolve that had defined her from the moment she had stepped foot onto his land.

But she had not told the tale of a broken man.

She had not stripped his past bare for the world to pick apart.

She had done something far more dangerous.

She had seen him.

Lucas read the passage again, his pulse thudding a slow, methodical beat against his ribs.

"I did not merely uncover a story in Dunster. I found a man who does not yet comprehend the weight of his own worth. A man who shields his heart from the world, and yet, gives more of himself than most men ever do. I left that place with one undeniable truth—Lucas Wycliffe is the kind of man one does not forget. The kind of man one does not stop caring for. The kind of man—one could love."

Could love.

The words settled into his chest, a quiet chisel against the wall he had spent years building.

Emma Ainsworth had never been his enemy.

She had never sought to betray him.

She had written the truth.

Not about his fall from grace. Not about his brother, nor the accident, nor the scandal that had chased him from the world he once knew.

But about him.

The man he had become. The life he had built. The worth he had long since abandoned.

She had seen him for more than his past.

And he—like a fool—had let her go.

❧

Lucas Wycliffe remained motionless upon the veranda, the sun sinking lower into the horizon, gilding the landscape with a golden hue. The familiar sights of Hawthorne Manor—the endless fields, the steady grazing of horses, the distant call of a lark—were unchanged.

And yet, they no longer felt like home.

Not without her.

For years, he had convinced himself that solitude was a choice. That by keeping his distance, by never asking for more, he was protecting himself from the inevitable losses life had always seemed to deal him.

But Emma Ainsworth had unraveled that lie with nothing more than her presence.

She had been a force of nature—storming into his life uninvited, pushing against his silence, refusing to accept his walls as immovable.

And now that she was gone, he felt the weight of her absence like an ache that settled deep within his chest, an emptiness that no amount of stubbornness could ignore.

He had spent days telling himself that she had been temporary, a fleeting interruption in the carefully ordered life he had built for himself.

But the truth—the godforsaken, undeniable truth—was that he had never felt more alive than when she had been near.

And now, he could not breathe at the thought of never seeing her again.

※

The sharp sound of boots against wood echoed across the quiet evening.

Lucas did not need to look up to know who it was.

Jacob Wycliffe stood at the edge of the porch, arms crossed, a knowing smirk playing at the corner of his lips.

"Been a long time since I've seen that look on your

face," Jacob drawled.

Lucas's jaw tensed. "What look?"

Jacob tilted his head slightly, as if he were regarding a man too foolish to recognize his own fate. "The 'I just lost the best damn thing that's ever happened to me' look."

Lucas exhaled sharply, rubbing a hand across his face. "It's not—"

Jacob let out a snort of disbelief. "Spare me, brother. I read the article."

Lucas's fingers tightened around the newspaper still resting on the table, its crisp edges slightly crumpled from where he had gripped it too hard.

"So did the whole damn village, apparently," he muttered, glancing toward the stables, where the stable-boys had been far too quiet around him all day. As if they knew something he didn't.

Jacob leaned against the railing, watching him closely. "Yeah. And you know what? It's the first time someone's told your story the way it was meant to be told. And you—like a stubborn fool—pushed her away for it."

Lucas's throat tightened. He did not answer.

Because Jacob was right.

Emma had written nothing but the truth. She had not exposed him, nor condemned him, nor painted him as anything other than a man who had tried to build something from the ruins of his past.

And what had he done?

He had let his fear ruin the one thing that had ever felt real.

Jacob shook his head, his voice quieter now. "You've been punishing yourself for five years, Lucas. Carrying this guilt around like it's some kind of penance. But Emma? She didn't see you as the man who failed." He motioned toward the paper still resting on the table. "She saw you as the man who kept going. The one who built something good. And you repaid her by letting her walk away."

Lucas swallowed against the tightness in his chest. "She deserved better."

Jacob scoffed. "No. She deserved the man she wrote about."

Lucas looked away, unable to meet his brother's gaze.

Because what if he wasn't that man?

What if Emma had seen something in him that did not exist?

Jacob exhaled, his tone measured now. "The question is—are you going to let her believe she was wrong about you? Or are you going to prove her right?"

Lucas remained still.

And for the first time in days, he felt something other than loss.

He felt purpose.

He knew what he had to do.

✿

The carriage rattled along the cobblestone street, its wheels rolling steadily toward the station. The morning was crisp, a pale mist clinging to the edges of the city, wrapping London in a quiet stillness.

Emma Ainsworth stood outside The Langham Hotel, her trunk at her side, her travel bag clutched in her gloved hand. The hem of her traveling gown swayed slightly in the cold breeze, but she barely noticed.

She was leaving.

Her fingers tightened around the handle of her bag.

It should have felt like a relief—boarding the train, returning to the life she had so carefully built for herself.

But all she felt was hollow.

She told herself it was for the best. That Lucas Wycliffe had made his choice, just as she had made hers. That the words she had written—the confession hidden between every carefully placed sentence—were all she had left to give.

And yet—

Her heart ached in a way she had never known before.

With a sharp inhale, she glanced down at her pocket watch.

Fifteen minutes.

Fifteen minutes, and she would be gone from this city. From him.

She took a deep breath and reached for her trunk, preparing to haul it into the carriage. The weight of it felt heavier than it should have. With every second that passed, her resolve weakened. What if he came? No—she couldn't allow herself that hope. Lucas didn't chase any-one. The clock ticked louder in her ears. Ten minutes now. Still no sign of him. Her heart clenched painfully as she turned toward the carriage door, preparing herself to leave for good.

Until—

The distant thunder of hooves upon stone shattered the quiet.

Emma turned, her breath catching as a familiar figure came into view.

Lucas.

Riding at full gallop through the morning mist, his coat billowing behind him, his expression fierce with something raw and unspoken.

Her heart leapt into her throat.

Because he had come.

And she was not too late.

Not yet.

❦

Lucas reined in his horse just feet from where she stood, his breath coming fast, his entire frame tense as though the very act of standing still was unbearable.

Emma froze. The world around her blurred, the bustling city noise fading into silence. Her heart beat so loudly she was certain it would drown out everything else.

She had imagined him chasing after her—had dreamed of it in the quiet hours of the night—but not like this. Not with such desperation in his eyes, not with every ounce of him screaming that this was his last chance.

For a long moment, neither of them spoke.

Emma could only stare.

He was disheveled, as though he had barely taken the time to dress before mounting his horse. His cravat was askew, his riding boots were covered in dust, and his dark hair—so often kept in strict order—was wild from the wind.

But his eyes—

His eyes burned into hers, full of something she had never seen before.

Something that stole the breath from her lungs.

"Lucas—"

"You cannot leave." His voice was hoarse, as though he had barely spoken the words aloud before now.

Emma swallowed hard. "I already have."

He shook his head, dismounting with a fluid grace before taking a step toward her. "No. You walked away because I gave you no choice. Because I was a fool. Because I was too damn scared to admit the truth."

Her heart pounded. "And what truth is that?"

Lucas exhaled, running a hand through his wind-tousled hair, his frustration evident. "That I love you."

Emma froze.

Lucas took another step, his hand reaching out—hesitant, as though afraid that one wrong move would send her running.

But she did not move.

She could not.

"I love you, Emma." His voice was rough, unsteady in a way that broke something deep inside her. "And I should have told you sooner. But I was afraid. Afraid that you would leave. Afraid that if I let myself want you, it would hurt too much when you were gone."

He swallowed hard, shaking his head. "But the truth is, you're already gone, and I have never known anything more unbearable."

Her throat burned. "Lucas—"

"I don't care about the past," he continued, his voice stronger now, fierce. "I don't care what I've lost, what I thought I had to protect myself from. None of it matters—not if it means losing you."

His hand cupped her cheek, his thumb brushing away the tear she had not realized had fallen.

"Stay," he murmured. "Please."

❦

Emma felt herself unravel.

Because this—this was not the same Lucas Wycliffe who had sent her away.

This was not the man who had hidden behind his walls, who had let his fears dictate his life.

This was the man she had fallen in love with.

A man who, for the first time, was standing before her completely unguarded.

Her hands trembled as she reached for him, her gloved fingers pressing against the rough stubble of his jaw.

Lucas closed his eyes, leaning into her touch, exhaling a breath that sounded like surrender.

She had spent so many nights wondering if this moment would ever come.

If he would ever fight for her.

If he would ever choose her.

And now—

Now, he had.

Emma let out a soft, breathless laugh, a sound that was equal parts joy and disbelief.

"Took you long enough."

Lucas's eyes flashed with something hot and undeniable.

And then—

She kissed him.

And Lucas Wycliffe, a man who had spent so many years believing that love was something lost to him—

Kissed her back like he was never letting her go.

Chapter Sixteen

The Dunster Harvest Fayre was in full flourish, the air alive with merriment, the gentle glow of lanterns casting a golden hue upon the cobblestone streets. Beneath the autumnal canopy of orange and gold, village people bustled about—laughter echoing as children darted between market stalls, the scent of roasted chestnuts and mulled wine weaving through the crisp evening air.

And yet, for Miss Emma Ainsworth, the revelry felt strangely distant.

She stood at the heart of the village square, encircled by familiar faces, bidding farewell to those who had, in such a brief span of time, become far more than mere acquaintances.

She had once believed herself to be a creature of the transient—one who belonged nowhere, a mere traveler of worlds, flitting from city to city, from tale to tale, never lingering long enough to be part of something permanent.

And yet, in Dunster, among these warm-hearted souls, she had found a place where she had belonged.

Perhaps not forever.

But for a fleeting, precious while.

She smiled tightly as Mrs.Pembroke, the ever-affectionate proprietress of the village bakery, took her hands in a gentle grasp, eyes crinkling with quiet understanding.

"Are you quite certain you must leave, dear heart?" the older woman inquired, a note of wistfulness in her tone. "A village such as ours could always find room for a writer with such a fine heart as yours."

Emma's throat constricted, her grip tightening around her travel case.

It would be so easy to say yes.

To stay.

To press herself into the fabric of this village, to allow its warmth to settle into her bones, to believe—if only for a little longer—that she could belong.

But she could not.

Not when she had already set her course.

Not when the one reason she might have truly stayed had not come.

The weight of unspoken words clawed at her chest. Every moment spent pretending she was ready to leave felt like another betrayal—to herself, to what she had felt in Lucas's arms. The memory of his voice, low and tender, haunted her more than she dared admit. But the empty space where he should have stood was louder than any confession could be. He wasn't here. And maybe… maybe that meant she had been wrong to hope in the first place.

She inhaled deeply, offering Mrs.Pembroke a small, practiced smile. "I think it is time," she murmured, the words tasting foreign upon her tongue.

Even as her heart rebelled.

Even as a treacherous part of her whispered, stay.

But staying for the village, for the kindness of its people, was not the same as staying for him.

And Lucas Wycliffe—

He was not here.

The breath she released was slow, measured. She adjusted the strap of her satchel, fingers curling tightly around the worn leather handle of her trunk.

This was it.

She turned.

Took one step.

Then—

A voice.

Deep, unmistakable.

"Emma!"

Her heart jolted violently in her chest. No—no, it couldn't be. She spun around too quickly, breath catching in her throat, eyes wide with disbelief. The din of the fayre faded into silence, replaced by the thunderous beat of her own pulse. This wasn't happening. It couldn't be him—

Her breath caught.

The fayre's bustle faded into a dull hum. The laughter, the music, the rustling of leaves ceased—as though the very air had stilled, waiting.

Emma turned, pulse roaring in her ears.

And there—at the farthest edge of the square, standing beneath the flickering glow of lantern light—was Lucas Wycliffe.

His greatcoat was undone, the fabric billowing slightly with the breeze, his breath still coming quick, as though he had ridden through half the night to reach her. His dark hair was windswept, his jaw shadowed with the beginnings of a beard, his stormy eyes locked onto hers with an intensity that rooted her to the spot.

But there was something different in him.

He no longer looked like a man on the verge of retreat.

He no longer carried the weight of unspoken regrets, nor the hesitation that had once been his shield.

No—this Lucas Wycliffe had come for her.

And this time—

He was not letting her go.

The fayre crowd had fallen into a hush, the murmur of voices dimming as though the very air held its breath. The village folk stood in clusters, their laughter stilled, their hands pausing over cider cups and sugared pastries as all eyes turned toward the man who had just spoken.

But Lucas Wycliffe did not see them.

Did not hear the whispers that rippled through the gathered assembly, nor notice the way the fayre lanterns flickered in the cool autumn breeze.

Because he only saw her.

Emma's pulse pounded in her ears, a wild, uneven rhythm that matched the riot of emotions surging through her chest.

Lucas walked toward her—not hurried, not hesitant, but with the quiet certainty of a man who had spent a lifetime keeping his distance, only to finally understand that some things were worth the risk.

Each step felt like a battle between hope and fear. His heart thundered in his chest, every breath thick with dread that he might be too late. The sight of her standing there—her eyes wide, her breath caught—stirred something deep inside him. He wanted to run, to close the distance and gather her into his arms. But she deserved more than desperation. She deserved certainty.

And then—

He stopped.

Close enough that she could feel the warmth radiating from him, close enough that she could see the storm of emotions shifting in his gaze.

But he did not touch her.

Not yet.

Emma swallowed hard, her voice barely more than a whisper. "Lucas, what are you doing?"

He exhaled, dragging a hand through his dark hair, his jaw tight with something that looked like both fear and reckless hope.

"I am attempting," he said, voice rough, "to fix the greatest mistake of my life."

A ripple of gasps stirred through the crowd.

Emma barely noticed.

Because Lucas Wycliffe was looking at her like she was the only thing in the world that mattered.

And for the first time—he was not holding back.

"I was wrong." His voice carried through the square, low and hoarse, yet steady. "I let my own fears, my past—my own damned pride—convince me that I did not deserve you. That if I let myself love you, I would lose you."

Emma's breath hitched.

The words struck her like a physical blow. Her throat tightened, and her vision blurred with unshed tears. Every wall she had built, every carefully constructed reason to leave—shattered in an instant. How was it possible for someone to break her heart and then mend it with nothing but a truth she had longed to hear?

Lucas stepped closer.

"But I do not care anymore." His voice cracked, his walls crumbling before her eyes. "I love you, Emma

Ainsworth. I love you, and I do not want you to leave. I do not want to watch you walk away, only to spend the rest of my life wondering if I let the best thing that ever happened to me slip through my fingers."

Emma's chest tightened so painfully she could scarcely draw breath.

She opened her mouth, heart roaring—but Lucas was not finished.

"I know I have no right to ask you to stay." He let out a breath, raw and unguarded, his eyes dark with emotion. "But I am asking anyway."

The air between them thickened, stretched, the weight of his words settling over her like a cloak.

The whole village was watching.

But for Emma, there was only him.

Lucas Wycliffe—the man she had fallen in love with.

The man who had, at last, stopped running.

❦

Emma's breath trembled in her chest. The fayre, the lanterns, the watching villages folk—all of it faded into a distant blur.

Because in this moment, there was only Lucas.

His confession hung in the air between them, raw and unguarded. He had given her his heart—laid it bare for her to either claim or refuse.

For so long, she had believed that love was not worth the risk. That attachments led to heartbreak, that promises shattered, that people left.

Perhaps that was still true.

But standing before this man, the weight of his gaze steady, unflinching, full of hope and fear in equal measure, Emma realized something else.

Perhaps—love was worth the risk after all.

A breath.

A step.

And then, she closed the space between them.

Her hand hovered in the air, trembling slightly. Could she trust this? Could she allow herself to believe that this wasn't just another cruel twist of fate? His gaze—raw, open, and utterly unguarded—silenced every doubt. This wasn't a man offering false promises. This was Lucas Wycliffe, stripped bare of fear, asking her to take the risk with him.

Her trembling fingers lifted, pressing against the firm expanse of his chest, feeling the strong, steady beat of his heart beneath her touch.

Lucas sucked in a sharp breath, his hands twitching at his sides as though holding himself back.

"Say something," he whispered, his voice rough, strained.

Emma exhaled, her lips curving—soft, certain, full of something new.

"It is about time, Mr. Wycliffe."

And then—she kissed him.

A moment of perfect, breathless silence.

Then—

An eruption of sound.

Gasps, cheers, the delighted laughter of village folk who had long suspected what Lucas Wycliffe himself had been too blind to see.

Somewhere, Mrs.Pembroke clapped her hands in delight.

Somewhere else, a voice called, "Took him long enough!"

And yet, Lucas heard none of it.

Because Emma Ainsworth was in his arms.

And he was never letting her go again.

The kiss was slow, deep, full of everything that had been left unsaid, of every moment they had wasted fighting this, denying this.

By the time they finally broke apart, laughter bubbled between them, breathless, incredulous, full of something wild and new.

Lucas rested his forehead against hers, his voice lower, rougher, tinged with something dangerously close to tenderness.

"So, does this mean you are staying?"

Emma's heart felt too full, too light, too impossible to contain.

She tilted her head, mischief glinting in her gaze.

"I suppose that depends."

Lucas raised a brow. "On what, precisely?"

She looped her arms around his neck, letting her fingers toy with the collar of his shirt, her smile slow, teasing.

"On whether or not you intend to kiss me like that every single day."

Lucas grinned slyly, the kind of smile that was entirely hers now, forever.

"Miss Ainsworth," he murmured, tipping her chin up once more, "you may count on it."

And when he kissed her again, with all the certainty of a man who knew exactly where he belonged—

Emma knew, without a shadow of a doubt—

She had finally found her home.

Chapter Seventeen

The first morning that Miss Emma Ainsworth awakened in Dunster as a woman who was not leaving, she experienced a most peculiar sensation—peace.

For the first time in many years, her thoughts were not consumed by her next destination, her next article, or the ceaseless rush of the world beyond this quiet village.

Instead, her thoughts were of him.

Of Lucas Wycliffe.

Of the man who had, before the entire village, declared that he loved her.

And of the fact that—at last—she had stayed.

Emma stretched beneath the warm weight of her blankets, the golden light of early morning spilling through the lace-curtained window of the small but cozy guest cottage at Hawthorne Manor.

She had expected that settling here would feel like an impossible leap—a departure from the life she had always known, the world she had so carefully crafted for herself.

But as she lay there, listening to the distant sounds of the horses in the paddock, the rustle of the wind through the tall grasses, the familiar cadence of boots crunching against gravel—

It did not feel like a sacrifice.

It did not feel like an ending.

It felt—like coming home.

And for the first time, she understood what it meant to stop running. This wasn't just the absence of motion—it was the presence of peace. The kind of stillness she had never allowed herself to feel, for fear it might tether her somewhere she didn't belong. But here, in Dunster—with Lucas—she had found something entirely unexpected. Not just a pause from the chaos, but a life she hadn't realized she was allowed to want.

And Lucas?

Lucas Wycliffe was the reason why.

The morning air was crisp as Emma struggled to lift a wooden pail of grain, her breath hitching slightly under the weight of it.

From his place against the paddock fence, Lucas watched her with infuriating amusement, arms crossed, the faintest smirk tugging at the corners of his mouth.

"You know, Ainsworth," he drawled, voice rich with unapologetic teasing, "I reckon that city life is gonna start wearing off you real quick."

Emma gritted her teeth, resisting the urge to throw the bucket at his head.

"Oh, do be quiet."

Lucas chuckled, his broad shoulders shaking slightly, his blue eyes alight with mischief.

"I'll admit, I half-expected you to retreat back to London after a week," he mused.

Emma shot him a glare of pure defiance, sweat forming at the nape of her neck. "You would have loved that, wouldn't you?"

Lucas feigned deep contemplation, tilting his head just so, his expression mockingly thoughtful.

"…Perhaps."

Emma exhaled sharply, lowering the heavy bucket onto the grass with a thud, placing her hands on her hips as she caught her breath.

"Just admit it, Lucas," she panted, brushing a stray strand of hair from her flushed cheeks. "You're impressed."

Lucas folded his arms across his chest, surveying her with a slow, deliberate gaze, as though weighing the notion carefully.

His eyes lingered a little longer than necessary—warmth flickering behind his teasing smirk. It wasn't just amusement that softened his gaze—it was something more. Something that saw her, not as a city outsider fumbling through country life, but as someone who belonged here. Someone who belonged with him.

"You've yet to collapse, so I suppose I'm… mildly astonished," he admitted at last, though his smirk betrayed his amusement.

Emma huffed, rolling her eyes—but she could not quite suppress her own smile.

It had been fortnight since she had unpacked her trunks and made her decision irrevocable.

And in that time, she had learned several things:

1. Rising before dawn to feed the horses was a form of exertion she had woefully underestimated.

2. The entire village had known of her and Lucas long before they themselves had fully come to terms with it.

3. Lucas Wycliffe found far too much delight in watching her struggle—and even more in pretending not to care.

And perhaps most surprising of all—

She loved every second of it.

❧

The evening air was crisp, carrying the scent of damp earth and wild heather as Emma sat curled upon the broad wooden porch of Lucas's rustic lodge. A woolen shawl was wrapped about her shoulders, shielding her from the chill, though she scarcely noticed the cold.

Before her stretched the vastness of Hawthorne , the

land bathed in the soft silver glow of moonlight, the world still and quiet save for the occasional rustling of the trees.

Lucas sat beside her, one arm draped lazily against the back of the bench, his posture relaxed in that way of his—a man accustomed to solitude, yet somehow content in her presence.

They had not spoken for some time.

And yet—it was not an uncomfortable silence.

Emma had spent her entire life filling pauses with words, believing that stillness signified something lacking, something uncertain.

But Lucas's silence—his silence was different.

It was steady, grounding, full.

It was a home she had never known she needed.

The silence between them wasn't just the absence of words—it was trust. The kind of trust that didn't demand constant reassurance, but instead existed in shared glances, gentle touches, and the unspoken understanding that they were exactly where they needed to be.

Lucas shifted slightly beside her, the warmth of him radiating in the cool night. His gaze flickered toward her, sharp yet gentle.

"Penny for your thoughts?"

Emma smiled faintly. "You wouldn't believe how cheap that is for me."

Lucas let out a low chuckle, the sound deep, familiar.

His fingers brushed lightly against hers where they rested upon the bench.

Emma's breath hitched.

Because for all the teasing, all the banter, all the defiance and stubbornness that had defined them in the beginning—this was different.

This was real.

She turned to him, studying the rugged lines of his face, the way the firelight from inside the cottage cast golden shadows along his features.

"Is this strange for you?" she asked softly.

Lucas frowned slightly. "What?"

"This." She hesitated. "Us. Having something… real. A true courtship."

She swallowed, her voice quieter now. "You were alone for a long time, Lucas."

Lucas said nothing for a moment.

Then, slowly—deliberately—he reached for her hand.

Lacing their fingers together.

Holding on.

"Aye," he admitted at last, his voice hushed, thoughtful. "It's strange."

Emma's heart clenched.

But before she could pull away, before she could let doubt settle in, he gave her hand a gentle squeeze.

"But it is also the finest damn thing that has ever happened to me."

Emma felt the sting of warmth rise to her eyes, her chest tightening beneath the weight of his words.

Her breath hitched, the vulnerability of his admission hitting her like a wave. This wasn't the brooding, guarded man she had first encountered—this was someone who had fought through his fear, lowered his defenses, and chosen her. And in that moment, every doubt, every lingering uncertainty melted away.

Lucas Wycliffe was not a man prone to grand declarations or poetic confessions.

But when he spoke—he meant every word.

And she knew, in that moment—she would never tire of hearing them.

That night, beneath the soft glow of candlelight, Lucas kissed her—slowly, deliberately—as though time itself had bent to his will, as though nothing and no one could pull them apart now.

And for the first time, Emma allowed herself to believe it.

There was no hurried desperation between them, no reckless, fleeting abandon.

This was something deeper. Something lasting.

They took their time.

Lucas moved with the patience of a man who had learned that some things in life—the right things—ought to be cherished, not rushed.

And Emma let herself memorize him.

Her fingertips traced the scars on his shoulders, the rough ridges of muscle along his back, the way his body told its own story—one of hardship, of resilience, of a man who had fought battles both seen and unseen.

And Lucas let her in.

Every touch became a conversation.

Every kiss—a promise.

By the time Emma lay curled against him, her cheek pressed to the solid warmth of his chest, she listened to the slow, steady beat of his heart and knew—without a single doubt—that she had found something she had never expected.

Love.

Not the kind built on infatuation.

Not the kind meant to be forgotten.

But the kind that endured.

And neither of them had any intention of letting it slip away.

✤

The following morning, as Emma strolled through the cobblestone streets of Dunster to purchase a cup of coffee, she noticed something peculiar.

The moment she stepped into the bakery, conversation halted.

Every eye turned toward her.

Mrs.Pembroke—flour-dusted and beaming—peered at her over the counter with the knowing smirk of a woman who had seen it all before.

Constable Tate, seated in the corner, lifted his coffee mug in her direction, a slow grin creeping across his face. "Well, well. Looks like Wycliffe finally made an honest woman out of you, Miss Ainsworth."

Emma promptly choked on air.

"Excuse me?" she sputtered, eyes wide.

The constable merely chuckled, while Mrs.Pembroke clapped her hands together, positively radiant with satisfaction.

"Oh, honey," she said, reaching across the counter to pat Emma's hand. "We all knew it was only a matter of time."

Emma narrowed her gaze. "What is it with this village?"

Mrs.Pembroke winked. "We pay attention, sweetheart."

Constable Tate quirked a brow. "And we're happy for you. That boy needed someone to pull him out of his shell."

Emma sighed, pressing her palm to her forehead. "This village is insufferable."

Mrs.Pembroke chuckled. "This village is home."

Emma opened her mouth to argue, to protest—but then, quite suddenly, she stopped.

Because the truth settled over her like a warm embrace.

She was no longer an outsider, merely passing through.

For the first time in her life, she belonged.

And it had nothing to do with her career.

It had everything to do with Lucas.

That evening, as the night stretched long and still around them, Emma nestled beneath the blankets, her body warm against Lucas's own.

The world outside was silent, save for the occasional rustling of the wind through the trees, the distant whinny of a horse in the paddock.

Lucas lay beside her, his arm draped over her waist, his breathing slow and even.

Emma traced small, idle patterns against the fabric of his shirt, her heart brimming with a quiet, unshakable contentment.

And then—in the dark, in the hush of their shared solitude—he spoke.

"I don't say it enough."

His voice was low, almost uncertain.

Emma blinked, sleepily shifting against him. "Say what?"

A pause.

Then, a breath.

"That I love you."

Emma's heart swelled.

She smiled against his chest, the warmth of his words settling into the very marrow of her bones.

She lifted her head slightly, whispering—soft and certain—"I love you too, yeoman."

Lucas exhaled, a small, contented sigh escaping him.

And as he pulled her closer, holding her like she was something precious, something irreplaceable, Emma realized—

This was no longer a temporary stay.

This was home.

This wasn't just comfort—it was something deeper, something permanent. Every heartbeat against his chest was a promise of shared mornings, quiet evenings, and laughter in between. She had found not just love, but the safety of being fully seen, fully known—and still completely accepted.

And she had no intention of leaving.

Chapter Eighteen

Lucas Wycliffe had never been a man to dwell upon the past.

Regret, he had long decided, was a burden best left untouched—a weight that served no purpose but to anchor a man to a life he could no longer change.

But regret, he realized now, wasn't about changing the past—it was about acknowledging the parts of yourself that still bled beneath old scars. Avoidance had been his shield, but shields could become cages. And Lucas was tired of being trapped by his own silence.

For five years, he had lived by that philosophy. He had poured himself into the work at Hawthorne, into the horses, into the land, convincing himself that forward was the only direction worth moving.

But then—Emma.

Emma, who had challenged him.

Emma, who had seen him for more than just his past. Emma, who had refused to let him keep running.

And now, for the first time in years, Lucas found himself looking backward—not with bitterness, but with the quiet, undeniable certainty that there were things he still needed to mend.

And it started with Jacob.

The morning air was crisp, the faint scent of earth and dew lingering over the pastures of Hawthorne . The sky, tinged with hues of soft lavender and pale gold, stretched endlessly above them as the quiet sounds of the estate stirred to life.

Lucas sat upon the porch, his gaze fixed upon the folded sheet of paper before him—a simple slip of parchment, yet one that held far more weight than its thin fibers should.

The letter.

He had been staring at it for the better part of an hour, as though the inked words upon its surface were some final verdict, a reckoning he was not yet prepared to face.

Beside him, Emma sat with a quiet patience that unsettled him as much as it comforted him.

Her bare feet were tucked beneath her, the soft folds of her dressing gown draped loosely over her frame as she cradled a porcelain cup of coffee in her hands. She sipped leisurely, watching him with those keen, knowing eyes—

the ones that saw far more than he ever spoke aloud.

"You could simply send a telegram," she murmured, breaking the silence, her voice warm with understanding.

Lucas let out a breath, rubbing a hand over the stubble on his jaw. "And say what?"

Emma shrugged. "That you're ready to speak to him."

Lucas exhaled sharply, his fingers tightening around the letter.

For years, he had avoided this—reaching out, reopening wounds that had long since been buried beneath silence. A telegram would be quicker, easier, but there were things that could not be said in the cold brevity of a few rushed lines.

No. If he was to do this, it had to be done properly.

Emma set her cup down and reached over, placing a hand atop his.

The warmth of her touch was grounding, steady—a reminder that he wasn't alone in this. That someone had chosen to stay, even when the parts of himself he most feared had been laid bare. It wasn't pity in her gaze, nor expectation. Just patience. And that, more than anything, terrified him.

"Whatever you write," she said softly, "he's been waiting to hear it."

Lucas swallowed hard, staring at the words before him.

And for the first time in years—he picked up the pen.

For years, Lucas Wycliffe had let silence serve as his only response.

Not for lack of opportunity. Jacob had reached out once or twice—brief, passing gestures that bore no expectations. An attempt, perhaps, at something resembling reconciliation.

And yet, Lucas had never answered.

Not because he did not wish to.

Not because he did not care.

But because he had not known how.

What words did a man offer to the brother whose dreams had shattered at his feet?

What apology could possibly mend what had been broken?

Lucas had carried the weight of that question for five long years.

And now, as he sat alone in the quiet solitude of his study, his fingers curled around the aged parchment before him, he knew there was only one way to find out.

The letter had arrived that morning, bearing his brother's name in a hand he had not seen in years.

He inhaled.

Broke the wax seal.

Unfolded the crisp sheet of paper, his pulse steady but his breath uneven.

And then—a voice from the past, captured in ink.

Lucas,

It took you long enough.

I won't lie—I wasn't sure I'd ever hear from you again. Thought maybe you had buried me along with everything else.

If you're finally ready to talk, I'm here.

Write me.

Or better yet—come see me.

Jacob

❧

They met in a small, unassuming establishment two villages over—a place where neither of them carried the weight of old memories.

Lucas had insisted upon it.

The thought of speaking these words while standing upon the land where everything had fallen apart—where Jacob had once dreamt, where he had once trained, where he had once believed—was too much.

Jacob was already there when Lucas arrived, seated at a corner booth by the window, arms crossed over his chest. The light from the street lamps cast faint shadows along his features, highlighting the subtle ways time had changed him.

Lucas hesitated for a fraction of a second before striding forward and sliding into the seat across from him.

Jacob studied him, his expression unreadable. Then, at last—"You look the same."

Lucas smirked. "You look older."

Jacob scoffed, shaking his head. "You're an ass."

Lucas let out a quiet chuckle, but the sound faded almost immediately.

Because the moment for pleasantries had passed. Because there was too much unsaid between them.

And because now—at long last—it was time to fix what had been broken.

✂

Jacob Wycliffe exhaled, his fingers idly tracing the rim of his untouched cup of coffee. He studied his brother for a long moment, the weight of the years between them settling heavily in the dimly lit corner of the establishment.

At last, he spoke.

"So why now, Lucas?"

Lucas did not have an easy answer.

So, he told the truth.

He lifted his gaze, his voice steady but quiet.

"Because I've got someone who won't let me keep running." He swallowed, his hands clenching into fists beneath the table. "Because I don't want to be that man anymore."

Jacob's expression shifted—just slightly. The tightness in his jaw eased, his shoulders relaxing as though he had been bracing himself for a different response entirely.

He nodded slowly, thoughtful.

Then, leaning back against the worn leather of the

booth, he murmured, "You know, I spent a long time being angry at you."

Lucas stiffened.

The words struck deep—far deeper than any accusation could have.

Jacob sighed, rubbing a hand over his face. "Not because of the accident."

The admission hit Lucas like a fist to the gut. He had built his entire life around the belief that his greatest sin was what had happened on that field—that Jacob's injury was the wound neither of them could mend. But now, sitting across from his brother, the truth was far worse: The real hurt had not been the fall. It had been the silence that followed.

Lucas's brows furrowed. "Then why?"

Jacob hesitated. Then, his jaw clenched, his voice rough with something unspoken.

"Because you disappeared."

Lucas looked away, a sharp pang twisting through his chest.

It was a simple truth, yet it carried the weight of everything they had left unsaid.

"I thought you hated me," Lucas admitted, his voice low.

Jacob let out a short, bitter laugh. "Hate you? Jesus, Lucas, you were my brother. You still are."

His fingers curled around the edge of the table, his

grip tight. "I never wanted you to disappear. I just wanted you to…" He let out a slow breath, searching for the right words. "I wanted you to let me be mad. To let me grieve it. But instead, you acted like the only way to fix it was to disappear."

Lucas stared at him.

The realization settled heavily in his chest, cold and undeniable.

All this time, he had believed he was carrying Jacob's pain for him—bearing the weight of it alone, protecting his brother from the burden.

But Jacob had never needed that.

He had never needed silence.

He had never needed distance.

He had never needed Lucas to atone for something they both had lost.

He had just needed his damn brother.

Lucas swallowed hard, the weight of that realization pressing into his chest like a stone. All this time, he thought guilt had been his way of carrying Jacob's pain for him—shielding him from the reminder of everything lost. But Jacob hadn't needed a martyr. He had needed a brother who was willing to stay in the wreckage and help rebuild.

Lucas exhaled sharply, rubbing a hand over the back of his neck. "I don't know how to fix this."

Jacob tilted his head, considering him for a long moment.

Then, at last, his lips quirked into a wry, knowing smile.

"Then I suppose it is fortunate that I never asked you to."

The clock in the distant village square chimed the hour, a solemn sound against the quiet hush of the countryside. Lucas Wycliffe sat across from his brother, a man he had not truly spoken to in years, and for the first time in an age, he did not feel like a man burdened by ghosts.

Their conversation meandered at first, circling around the unspoken truths like men wary of waking a sleeping beast. But eventually, they spoke—really spoke.

Jacob recounted tales of his new life, of the farm he had begun tending, of the wounded riders he had dedicated himself to helping, men who had been thrown by fate as surely as he once had been.

Lucas, in turn, told of the estate, of the horses, of the life he had carved from ruin with his own hands. And then—when he could no longer skirt the subject—he spoke of her.

At the mention of Emma Ainsworth, Jacob leaned back against his chair, his expression laced with amusement.

"This woman of yours," he said with a knowing grin. "She must be remarkable if she managed to bring you out of hiding."

Lucas, shaking his head. "You have no idea."

Jacob studied him for a long moment, then, voice softer, asked, "And what do you intend to do about her?"

Lucas exhaled, his gaze dropping to his hands, calloused from years of work, steady from years of restraint. He had spent so long convincing himself that love was something he could not afford—that it was a risk, a weakness, a tether to a past he had wanted to escape.

But now, looking up at his brother, feeling the weight of reconciliation settle between them, he knew the answer.

At long last, he lifted his gaze, a rare, genuine smile tugging at the corner of his lips.

"I intend to keep her."

Not just to love her—but to build something with her. A life not defined by the shadows of the past but illuminated by the possibility of what could be. With Emma, it wasn't about redemption. It was about finally allowing himself to believe that he deserved more than loneliness.

⁂

The evening air was crisp as Lucas returned to Hawthorne Manor, the great estate bathed in the golden remnants of twilight. The world felt still, the hum of insects and distant rustle of horses the only sounds to greet him.

But as he ascended the steps to the wide wooden porch, he found the only sight that truly mattered.

Emma was waiting for him.

She sat with a book in her lap, a woolen shawl draped over her shoulders, her tea cooling on the table beside her. The glow of the lantern beside her flickered, casting golden hues against her soft features.

She did not ask how the conversation had gone.

She did not need to.

Instead, she reached out, her fingers brushing his in quiet understanding.

Lucas took her hand, his grip firm, steady, as though anchoring himself to something he had been searching for far longer than he had ever admitted.

For the first time in years, he was no longer alone. For the first time in years, he was not a man running from the past, but one walking toward the future.

He had made amends with his brother. And here, before him, was the woman he had no intention of letting slip away.

❧

Lucas stood on the porch of Hawthorne , the night air cool against his skin, the distant sounds of the estate settling around him like a familiar song. The world had not changed. The land was still the same, the stars still stretched endlessly overhead, the scent of horses and earth still thick in the breeze.

But he had changed.

For the first time in years, the weight in his chest wasn't something he had to bear alone. He had spoken to Jacob. They had confronted the past, not with anger, not with blame, but with understanding. And for the first time in far too long, Lucas had his brother back.

And he had Emma.

She was waiting for him now, standing at the doorway, arms crossed, watching him with that quiet patience of hers. She had known this conversation with Jacob would leave him raw, had known he needed time to sort through it all before he could find the words to tell her.

But she had never once doubted that he would.

Lucas turned to her, stepping forward until they were close enough for him to reach out, to slide his hands over her waist, to feel the warmth of her beneath his fingertips. Emma searched his face, her gaze soft, steady.

There was no pressure in her eyes, no expectation for him to be anything other than exactly what he was. Just a quiet promise that she would stand beside him, no matter how messy the healing process became.

"How do you feel?" she asked, her voice low.

Lucas let out a breath. "Lighter."

Her lips curled in a small smile. "Good."

He tucked a strand of hair behind her ear, his touch lingering. "I was wrong before," he murmured.

Emma's brows lifted. "About what?"

His fingers brushed over her cheek, his voice rough, unguarded. "About thinking I didn't deserve this."

Emma exhaled, something flickering in her expression. She pressed a hand over his heart, her touch grounding, solid. "You always did, Lucas."

His throat tightened.

For so long, he had believed that the past defined him. That what had happened to Jacob, what had happened to his career, was a burden he had to carry alone. That letting anyone in would only lead to more loss.

But Emma had proven him wrong.

She had stayed.

She had fought for him even when he had pushed her away.

And he wasn't going to waste another second pretending he didn't want the life she had made him believe was possible.

Lucas leaned down, pressing his forehead against hers, his breath mingling with hers in the quiet of the night. "I love you, Emma Ainsworth."

She smiled, tilting her chin up, her lips brushing against his. "I love you too, Lucas Wycliffe."

And as he kissed her—slow, deep, full of all the things he had never been able to say before—Lucas knew one thing with absolute certainty.

This was home.

And he wasn't running anymore.

Lucas stood on the porch, letting the weight of the evening settle over him. The sky was darkening, a deep indigo stretching wide over the rolling hills, the scent of fresh hay and earth thick in the cooling air. The world felt quieter now—not empty, not lonely. Just… still.

Emma didn't speak, didn't press him for details. She simply stood beside him, offering warmth without asking for anything in return. He could feel the steady beat of her heart through the space between them, the unspoken understanding in the way she waited.

For years, Lucas had believed that some wounds never fully healed—that you just learned to live around them, to carry them like old scars. But sitting across from Jacob today, hearing his brother's voice, seeing the forgiveness in his eyes, Lucas had realized something.

Maybe healing wasn't about forgetting. Maybe it was about learning how to move forward anyway.

Emma tugged lightly on his hand, pulling him toward the steps. "Come inside," she murmured, her voice soft, steady. "You look like you could use a drink."

Lucas huffed a quiet laugh. "You offering whiskey?"

Emma grinned. "I was thinking tea. But if you need something stronger, I won't judge."

He let her lead him inside, let the warmth of the house wrap around him. And as he watched her move through the kitchen, pouring tea into two mugs, humming softly to herself, he felt something settle deep in his chest.

This was what home felt like.

Not just the land, not just the estate, not just the work he had built with his own two hands.

But her.

Emma turned, catching him staring, raising an amused brow. "What?"

Lucas shook his head, taking the mug from her, letting his fingers brush against hers. "Nothing."

She studied him for a second, eyes knowing. "You're different."

He took a slow sip of tea, nodding. "Yeah. I think I am."

Emma smiled. "Good."

Lucas exhaled, his grip tightening around the mug. "Jacob's coming to visit next month."

Surprise flickered across her face, followed quickly by something softer. "That's… really good, Lucas."

He nodded. "Yeah. It is."

They stood there in the quiet, the weight of the past no longer pressing quite so hard.

And for the first time in a long, long time—Lucas Wycliffe felt like a man who wasn't just surviving.

He wasn't defined by what he had lost. Not by the fall, not by Jacob's injury, and not by the years spent in silence. What defined him now was choice—the choice to stay, to forgive, to love without reservation. And as he looked toward Emma, his future stretched before him, vast and full of possibilities.

He was living.

✿

Chapter Nineteen

The dawn light spilled through the windows of Hawthorne Manor, golden and gentle, illuminating the modest kitchen where Emma sat, fingers poised above her open journal. A fresh cup of coffee sent delicate tendrils of steam curling into the air, its rich aroma mingling with the scent of aged wood and the faint, lingering traces of last night's rain.

Across from her, Lucas leaned against the counter, arms crossed, his gaze unreadable. The morning had been quiet between them—easy, familiar—but now, something unspoken thickened the air between them.

She met his eyes. "I received an offer."

Lucas's posture straightened, his expression giving nothing away, though Emma could sense the shift in him.

"An offer?" he repeated, his voice measured.

Emma hesitated only for a moment before turning the journal toward him, the crisp parchment bearing the weight of a letter she had received just that morning.

"The magazine I used to work with," she explained, tapping the page lightly. "They've asked me to take on a full feature series—traveling to small villages, writing about the people who make them special."

Lucas's stomach tightened, the words sinking deep, twisting in a way he didn't care for.

Travel.

Which meant leaving.

He forced himself to nod, his voice even. "That's a huge opportunity."

Emma studied him carefully. "It is."

A silence stretched between them, long and heavy.

Then—she sighed. "But…"

Lucas swallowed, trying to ignore the way his throat felt too tight, his chest too heavy. "But it's not here."

Emma's gaze softened, her fingers idly tracing the rim of her cup. "No," she admitted. "It's not."

Lucas sat back, the truth sinking in like a stone tossed into still water. Every rational part of him knew he should let her go if that's what she needed—encourage her to chase her dreams, even if it meant carving her absence into the walls of his world. But the selfish part? The part that had learned how to breathe again because of her? That part ached at the thought of losing her.

Lucas could feel the words pressing against his ribs, the ones he didn't know how to say—the ones that felt too selfish to speak aloud.

He had no right to ask her to stay.

No right to stand in the way of her dreams.

But the thought of her leaving—of waking up to a world where she wasn't beside him, where her laughter wasn't echoing through the estate, where he wasn't pulling her into his arms after a long day—it was unbearable.

He forced himself to keep his voice steady. "Do you want to take it?"

Emma hesitated.

And that hesitation sent a flicker of hope through him.

She had wanted this once.

A career. A life beyond the borders of a small village.

But now?

She looked torn.

Finally, she sighed, running a hand through her hair. "I don't know."

Lucas exhaled slowly. "You should."

Emma's head snapped up, eyes widening. "What?"

Lucas shifted, his jaw tight. "If it's what you want— you should go."

Emma stared at him, her expression unreadable, her

fingers curling into her lap.

And Lucas wondered if he had just made the biggest mistake of his life.

The quiet that followed was different from the comfortable silences they had come to share. This one was heavier—weighted with something unspoken, something fragile.

Lucas stood motionless, his arms still crossed over his chest, though his grip had tightened, his knuckles paling. His world had been built on the certainty of things—the changing of seasons, the steady rhythm of work, the land beneath his feet.

But Emma Ainsworth had never been something certain.

She had been unexpected. A force of nature, walking into his life with ink-stained fingers and a sharp wit, with eyes that saw straight through him. She had upended his world in the best way. And now, she had the chance to leave.

A chance she had earned.

"I suppose," he said, forcing the words out, "you've already decided."

Emma's brow furrowed, her lips parting, but she hesitated. And that hesitation sent a flicker of something dangerous through him.

Doubt.

Hope.

"No," she admitted. "I haven't."

Lucas exhaled slowly, his gaze never leaving hers. "Why not?"

Emma stared down at her coffee cup, her fingers running along the rim. "Because… I don't know if that's what I want anymore."

Lucas's heart pounded once, hard.

He should be relieved. But instead, all he felt was fear.

Because he knew what he wanted.

But he also knew that Emma Ainsworth was not the kind of woman who could be contained.

And the last thing he wanted was for her to stay—only to regret it.

✤

Emma set her notebook aside and stood, moving toward him. "Lucas."

Emma's heart pounded against her ribs like a warning. Every step she took toward him felt like walking a tightrope—one wrong word, one misstep, and the fragile foundation they had built could shatter. But she couldn't leave this question unspoken. Not now. Not when every fiber of her being was screaming for him to give her a reason to stay.

He swallowed. "Yeah?"

She hesitated, her gaze searching his. "Do you want me to stay?"

The question was so quiet, so simple—and yet, it struck him like a blow.

He could lie.

Could tell her that her dreams were more important than his own selfish wants. That he would never ask her to give up the future she had worked so hard to build.

But he had spent too many years hiding from the truth.

And Emma Ainsworth deserved more than that.

His jaw tightened. "Yeah."

Her breath caught, her eyes darkening.

"I do."

He reached for her then, his fingers brushing her arm, tentative, as if he wasn't sure whether she would pull away.

She didn't.

Instead, she exhaled shakily, closing the last bit of space between them.

"I don't want to go," she whispered.

Lucas swallowed against the tightness in his throat.

"Then don't."

The words were simple, rough—but they carried more weight than anything he had ever said.

Because they weren't just words.

They were a promise.

✤

The evening air was crisp with the lingering warmth of

the sun, the sky a tapestry of gold and indigo as twilight settled over Hawthorne . Lucas and Emma sat upon the back porch, the scent of fresh earth and hay drifting through the breeze, mingling with the quiet hum of insects in the distance.

Lucas had never been a man for grand gestures, nor for poetic words, but there was something profoundly right about this moment—about her, here, beside him.

His arm rested lazily along the back of her chair, their fingers entwined in a manner that felt easy, natural, as if they had been made to fit just so.

Emma exhaled, a contemplative sound, the kind that told him her mind was working through something.

Lucas quirked a brow. "I can hear you thinking."

Emma shot him a look, though there was no real heat behind it. "You make it sound like a dangerous activity."

He shrugged, the corner of his mouth lifting. "Depends on what you're thinking about."

She nudged his leg with her foot before settling back against her seat, watching the last streaks of pink fade from the horizon.

After a long pause, she murmured, "I don't have to take every assignment."

Lucas turned to her fully, brows lifting slightly. "No?"

Emma shook her head, her fingers tightening around his. "No. I can write from anywhere. And I want to write from here."

The decision had been clawing at her for days, a storm of doubt and fear. But in this moment—watching Lucas look at her as though she were the anchor to his entire world—everything settled into perfect, terrifying clarity. Her dreams didn't belong in crowded cities or distant headlines anymore. They belonged here. With him.

Something inside him—something long buried, long restrained—unclenched at her words.

"You're sure?" he asked, voice quieter than before, as if afraid to jinx the moment.

Emma turned, her expression steady, certain. "I've never been more sure of anything."

Lucas swallowed, then leaned in, pressing a kiss against her temple.

She was staying.

Not because she had to. Not because she had nowhere else to go.

But because she wanted to.

And for a man who had spent years believing that nothing good ever lasted—this felt like a miracle.

Emma smiled against his shoulder, exhaling contentedly.

"I am," she whispered.

And just like that—the future, which had once felt so uncertain, became something he could finally see.

Something worth building.

Something worth keeping.

Emma stepped out of the general shop, a bag of supplies balanced on her hip—only to freeze when she saw the man standing in front of her.

Her stomach twisted.

Nathan Reed.

Her former editor. And, briefly, her biggest mistake.

"Well, well," Nathan drawled, smirking. "Still playing at country life?"

She squared her shoulders. "What are you doing here?"

Nathan held up a copy of The London Observer—her article. "Came to see what all the fuss was about. Thought I'd pay you a visit. And, maybe, offer you a deal."

Emma frowned. "What deal?"

Nathan slid a business card from his coat pocket. "Your latest piece has everyone talking. The board wants you back, Emma. You'd have full creative control. No more small-village fluff. We're talking real investigative work—global stories, hard-hitting journalism."

Emma hesitated.

For a split second, she remembered the thrill of the chase, the rush of a high-profile assignment.

Then—she thought of Lucas. Of the estate. Of the life she had built here.

Nathan saw the hesitation. He smirked. "Don't tell me you're actually considering staying?"

Before she could answer, a familiar voice rumbled behind her.

"She's staying."

Lucas's voice was low but steady—a blade wrapped in velvet, cutting through any doubts that might have lingered. This wasn't a plea. It was a promise. One that said she wasn't just someone passing through—she was home.

She turned to find him standing there, arms crossed, eyes cold and steady.

Nathan arched a brow. "Ah. The horseman."

Lucas didn't blink. "The fiancé."

Emma's breath caught. What?

Nathan's smirk faltered. "Oh?"

Lucas stepped closer, his hand sliding around Emma's waist. "You're wasting your time, Reed. She's got a life here. One that doesn't involve chasing headlines for men who don't respect her."

Nathan's expression tightened. Then, with a sigh, he shook his head. "Your loss, Ainsworth."

He turned, tipping his hat as he walked away.

Emma exhaled slowly, staring after him.

Then—she turned to Lucas. "Fiancé?" she repeated, arching a brow.

Lucas shrugged. "Seemed easier than explaining everything."

Emma grinned slyly, wrapping her arms around his neck. "Well. Now you have to make an honest woman out of me."

Lucas grinned. "I plan on it."

And then—he kissed her.

One week had passed since Emma had chosen to stay—since Lucas had let himself believe that love was not something to fear, but something to hold onto.

Now, as he stood outside the guesthouse, hands buried deep within his pockets, he felt the unfamiliar weight of nerves settling low in his stomach. It was an odd sensation, unsettling yet exhilarating all the same.

When Emma stepped out onto the porch, the golden light of morning casting a warm glow over her, she tilted her head, studying him with a knowing smirk.

"Why do you look like you're about to tell me something life-changing?"

Lucas exhaled, smirking right back. "Because I am."

Emma arched a brow. "Should I sit down?"

Lucas shook his head, stepping forward, reaching for her hand. "Come with me."

No questions. No hesitation.

She simply followed.

Lucas's pulse quickened as they approached the clearing. Every step toward the cottage felt like walking toward a future he had never dared to imagine. What if she didn't like it? What if it wasn't enough? The weight of what this gift represented settled heavily on his shoulders—this wasn't just a cottage. It was a promise of permanence.

They walked in silence, past the main house, past the barn where the scent of fresh hay lingered in the air, past the paddock where the horses grazed idly in the morning sun.

And then—he stopped.

Before them stood a newly built cottage, modest yet welcoming, with a wraparound porch and large windows that reflected the endless blue of the sky.

Emma frowned, glancing between him and the structure before them. "What is this?"

Lucas shifted, rubbing the back of his neck—a telltale sign of nerves if Emma had ever seen one.

"You said you needed a place to write." He gestured toward the porch, the perfectly placed desk visible through the doorway, the sturdy walls built with intention. "So I built you one."

Emma's breath hitched, her lips parting, her eyes wide with disbelief.

She turned to him slowly, voice barely above a whisper. "Lucas…"

He swallowed hard, holding her gaze with steady resolve. "I want you here, Emma. Not just as a visitor. Not just for a little while." He exhaled, his fingers tightening around hers. "I want you to make a home here. With me."

Emma stared at him, something soft and fragile flickering in her expression.

"You built me cottage?"

Lucas smirked. "I had some help."

Emma let out a watery laugh, covering her mouth with her hands, her shoulders trembling with something between shock and sheer, overwhelming joy.

Her heart felt as though it might burst—this wasn't just a gift of space. This was Lucas giving her a future, laying down roots and asking her to be part of the life he had built, the life she had unknowingly become essential to. And in that moment, every doubt, every fear, every lingering hesitation dissolved.

Then, suddenly—she launched herself into his arms.

Laughing. Crying. Kissing him all at once.

Lucas caught her easily, wrapping his arms around her as she buried her face in his neck, whispering against his skin—

"God, I love you."

Lucas closed his eyes, his chest tightening with something fierce, something deep and undeniable.

He pulled back just enough to look at her, brushing her damp cheek with his thumb, his voice rough with emotion.

"Good. Because I love you too."

And as he kissed her beneath the endless sky, as she melted into him, as he held onto her like she was the only thing that had ever truly mattered—

Lucas Wycliffe knew.

He had made the right choice.

Because she was his future.

And he wasn't letting her go.

But she was more than just his future—she was his partner, his equal, the woman who had seen every flaw, every scar, and loved him not despite them, but because of them. Together, they weren't just surviving—they were building something extraordinary. A home. A life. A love that would endure.

And for the first time, Lucas Wycliffe wasn't afraid of what came next.

Chapter Twenty

One Year Later

The village of Dunster remained unchanged in many ways—the golden fields still stretched endlessly toward the horizon, the village square still bustled with laughter and warm familiarity, and the sound of horse hooves against soft earth still echoed across Hawthorne Manor every morning.

But Emma had changed.

She stood at the edge of the paddock, arms folded atop the worn wooden fence, watching as the last slivers of the sun cast their glow over the land. The sky burned in hues of gold and crimson, fading into the cool embrace of twilight. A gentle breeze stirred the air, rustling the wildflowers at her feet.

This had once been Lucas's world.

Now, it was theirs.

Never in her life had she imagined herself here—in a small village, rooted in a place where people knew her name, where she woke to the scent of fresh air and the distant murmur of horses rather than the relentless hum of city traffic.

But here she was.

And she had never been happier.

It wasn't just happiness—it was peace, the kind that came from knowing she had found where she truly belonged. Not in the noise of ambition or the endless rush of deadlines, but in the quiet certainty of shared mornings, whispered promises, and a love that had grown not in haste, but in steady, enduring devotion.

Emma's fingers traced the worn wood of the fence as she watched Lucas move effortlessly in the paddock, leading a newly rescued mare to the center of the enclosure.

The past year had seen the expansion of Hawthorne's rehabilitation program. What had once been a modest estate had grown into a haven for abandoned and injured horses, a place where second chances weren't just given— they were earned.

Lucas had thrown himself into the work, dedicating his days to the animals who needed him, to the people who came to learn from him.

And Emma had been beside him through all of it.

She had found her own rhythm here, setting up a

small office in the writing cottage Lucas had built for her, turning it into a place where she could write about the world—but always return home to him.

As she watched him now, the steady patience in his movements, the quiet confidence in his stance, Emma felt something warm and familiar swell in her chest.

This was the man she had fallen in love with.

The man who had once tried to push her away.

The man who had, finally, let her in.

He was no longer just a man haunted by his past—he was someone who had faced his fears and chosen love over solitude. Every step they had taken together had been a lesson in trust, in surrender, and in building something neither of them had dared to hope for.

Lucas glanced up, meeting her gaze.

For a moment, the world felt still.

And then—he smiled.

Not the small, almost imperceptible smirk he had given her when they first met.

Not the careful, hesitant grin of a man who was still learning how to let someone close.

A real smile.

And, God help her, she loved that smile.

❦

She had never stopped writing.

But instead of chasing stories across the country, she had begun capturing the world right here—in Dunster, in the rolling fields of Hawthorne Manor, in the quiet moments that told their own kind of story.

Her column on village life had become a beloved feature, drawing readers from every corner of the country. People sought out her words, longing for the simplicity, the second chances, the kind of steadfast love and purpose that could be found beyond the city lights.

And it had all begun with Lucas.

Her notebook lay open on the porch, the latest article half-finished. A gentle evening breeze rustled the pages. From the distance, she could hear the faint sound of laughter from the stable-boys, the soft rustling of the horses, the unmistakable footsteps of the man who had changed everything.

This was her life now.

And she would not trade it for anything in the world.

❦

That night, Emma sat curled up on the porch of her writing cottage—the very one Lucas had built for her with his own hands.

The night sky stretched wide above them, a sea of stars flickering like embers in the dark. The air was cool, crisp, carrying the lingering scent of fresh hay and distant rain.

Lucas's footsteps sounded on the wooden planks before she saw him. He carried two cups of coffee, the steam curling into the night air.

Wordlessly, he handed one to her.

Emma smiled, her fingers brushing against his as she took it. "Thank you."

Lucas settled onto the bench beside her, his body warm against hers.

They sat in companionable silence, listening to the quiet hum of the world around them, the gentle rustling of the wind, the distant call of an owl from the trees beyond the paddock.

Then, after a long moment, Lucas spoke.

"I read your latest article."

Emma turned, arching a brow. "You did?"

Lucas nodded, taking a slow sip of coffee. "It was good."

Emma smirked, the teasing light in her eyes unmistakable. "That's high praise from Lucas Wycliffe."

Lucas let out a soft huff of laughter, shaking his head. "It was more than good." His blue gaze held hers, something quiet but certain flickering in his expression. "You're really staying."

Emma set her coffee down and turned to face him fully. "I'm really staying."

Lucas exhaled, a long, slow breath, as if he had been waiting for those words all over again.

And then, without hesitation, he leaned in.

His lips met hers in a slow, deep kiss—one full of quiet promises, of forever, of home.

And Emma melted into him, knowing with absolute

certainty—

She had finally found where she belonged.

The morning air was crisp, the scent of damp earth and fresh hay lingering as the golden light of dawn crept over Hawthorne Manor.

Emma stretched beneath the warmth of the blankets before realizing that Lucas was not beside her.

Frowning, she pushed herself up, glancing out the window.

And there he was.

Pacing.

His broad form moved back and forth near the paddock, hands on his hips, his head tilted downward in deep thought.

Lucas Wycliffe was not a man prone to nervous pacing.

Something was going on.

Throwing on a sweater, Emma stepped outside onto the porch, her bare feet cool against the wood. She crossed her arms and smirked.

"Alright, warden. Spill."

Lucas turned at the sound of her voice, his lips quirking slightly—but there was something unreadable in his expression.

He rubbed the back of his neck, an old tell of his. "Come with me."

Emma arched a brow. "Should I be worried?"

Lucas grinned, stepping toward her, reaching for her hand. "Always."

They walked across the estate, the morning mist curling along the edges of the fields. The horses stirred in the paddock, their soft huffs breaking the early quiet.

Lucas led her toward the edge of the property, toward the rolling hill that overlooked the land.

And then—she saw it.

A construction site.

The outline of a small foundation already set in the earth, wooden beams stacked neatly to the side, tools carefully placed nearby.

Emma stopped short, her breath catching.

She turned to Lucas, her heart pounding. "Lucas… what is this?"

Lucas didn't hesitate. He turned toward her, his gaze steady, unwavering. "Our home."

Emma stared at him, the words settling deep into her chest. "Our…?"

Lucas nodded, stepping closer. "You love your writing cottage." His voice was steady, low. "But I figured you might want something… bigger. Something that's ours."

Emma covered her mouth, her breath shaking.

Lucas cupped her face gently, his calloused fingers warm against her skin. "You're not just a visitor here,

Emma. You never were." His blue eyes softened. "You're part of this place. And I want to build something with you. Not just a house. A life."

It wasn't just about the land or the house—it was about the future they were choosing to build together. A place filled with laughter, quiet mornings, shared burdens, and the kind of love that didn't need to be spoken to be understood.

Emma let out a watery laugh, tears burning behind her eyes.

She didn't need to think. Didn't need to question.

This was home.

Throwing her arms around his neck, she buried her face in his shoulder, laughing, crying, holding him tight.

"I love you."

Lucas exhaled, pressing his forehead against hers, his own breath a little uneven. "I love you too, Ainsworth."

And as they stood there, in the place where their future was about to be built, Emma knew—

Forever had never felt so real.

❧

The evening air was cool, tinged with the fading warmth of the sun, as Emma and Lucas walked along the paddock fence, their hands loosely intertwined. The sky was a canvas of deep gold and soft lavender, the last breath of daylight stretching over the horizon.

The world around them was quiet—the kind of quiet

that came when everything finally felt right.

Lucas slowed his steps, reaching into his pocket.

"Here," he said, holding out a small object.

Emma frowned, tilting her head. "What's this?"

Lucas smirked, that slow, knowing smirk that always made her pulse skip. "Open it."

Emma took the small box, lifting the lid with careful fingers.

Inside, nestled against dark velvet, was a delicate silver pendant—shaped like a horseshoe.

Her breath caught, her fingertips tracing the smooth curve of the charm.

"Lucas…" she whispered, her voice barely carrying over the rustling grass.

He reached up, tucking a strand of hair behind her ear. "It's not an engagement ring."

Emma arched a brow, the corner of her lips twitching. "No?"

Lucas exhaled, shaking his head. "Not yet."

Her heart stilled.

Not yet.

His blue eyes held hers, steady, unwavering. "But it's a promise."

Emma swallowed hard, the weight of his words pressing against her chest. "A promise?"

Lucas nodded, brushing his thumb over her knuckles.

"That we're not just a moment. That we're not temporary." He paused, his voice quieter now, more certain. "That I'm all in."

Emma closed her eyes for a moment, steadying herself against the rush of emotions.

This wasn't a fleeting moment of passion—it was the culmination of every second they had fought for each other. It was the promise of every sunrise shared, every challenge faced hand in hand, every ordinary day made extraordinary by the simple fact that they faced it together.

And then—she stepped closer.

Lifting onto her toes, she pressed a soft, lingering kiss to his lips, her answer sealed in the warmth of that single moment.

When she pulled away, her smile said everything she didn't need to say out loud.

Because she was all in, too.

The stars began to scatter across the sky, a thousand tiny lanterns lighting the night.

Lucas pulled her into his arms, resting his chin lightly atop her head, and Emma sighed against his chest, listening to the steady rhythm of his heart.

This was home.

Not a city. Not a career. Not the rush of deadlines or the chase of something more.

This. Him. Them.

And for the first time in forever, neither of them was running.

Because they had already found where they belonged.

It wasn't just a promise of forever—it was the quiet certainty of every ordinary moment they would share. The mornings spent wrapped in blankets, the laughter over forgotten cups of coffee, the steady comfort of shared silences. This was more than love—it was belonging. A life built not from grand gestures, but from the everyday magic of simply being together.

And forever started now.

...

www.ingramcontent.com/pod-product-compliance
Lightning Source LLC
Chambersburg PA
CBHW051820150726

47998CB00001B/224